AF441321

A Divisive Storm

A Dora Ellison Mystery

Book 6

A Divisive Storm
A Dora Ellison Mystery
Book 6

First Edition

By David E. Feldman

Copyright © 2023 David E. Feldman
All Rights Reserved

No part of this publication may be reproduced, distributed, or transmitted in any form or by any means, including photocopying, recording, or other electronic or mechanical methods, without the prior written permission of the publisher, except in the case of brief quotations embodied in reviews and certain other non-commercial uses permitted by copyright law.

This is a work of fiction. Unless otherwise indicated, all the names, characters, businesses, places, events, and incidents in this book are either the product of the author's imagination or used in a fictitious manner. Any resemblance to actual persons, living or dead, or actual events is purely coincidental.

For Matt & Cindy, with love

Table of Contents

Prologue

And there he was.

I knew where he'd be. I knew of several places he would be and times he would be at there. I had all the information. All I had to do was wait for the right opportunity. An empty parking lot or a busy street. Either might do, if they were right.

I'd know. I had lived for this.

The parking lot was all but empty. A few cars. No people.

I approached the car I'd spent so long looking for and smiled when I saw he was behind the wheel. He looked different, but the changes that came with age were superficial. The gray hair, the wrinkles, the heavier face (and probably the belly), and whatever other changes that came with time, couldn't hide the fact that all my hard work had paid off. I'd found him.

He saw me and smiled at first, not knowing who I was, and rolled down his window. When he glanced up again I saw recognition but not awareness. He knew me but didn't understand what I was doing there.

I watched the process, as if in slow motion. He knew the person behind these different, aged features, just as I knew him. The difference was I had context. I knew who he was, why he was in front of me, and what he'd done to deserve what was about to happen.

He had no idea.

At first.

Then it began to dawn on him. It took only seconds, but his benevolent smile faded into awareness as he remembered. An oh-so-brief confusion followed. What was I doing here, at his car window of all places?

He smiled a little at the memory at first, for just a fraction of a second—which made the terror that followed all the more rewarding. Because then he knew.

The terror was a big part of my reason for being here.

And I said one word—the word I had waited to say. "Justice."

All he said was, "Please!"

Then I put the gun against his cheek and shot him in the face. That was the other part of my reason for being here.

Best damn moment of my life.

Chapter 1

Dora Ellison awoke from yet another nightmare, once again fighting that violent assassin who had not so long ago nearly killed her. That near-death experience had wounded her deeply, and her energy was depleted. She was having trouble getting her five-foot-eight, one-hundred-forty-pound frame out of bed in the morning and had been having persistent panic attacks and nightmares.

PTSD and trauma, Missy called it, and insisted that Dora see a psychiatrist, who prescribed an antidepressant.

Missy was sitting in a chair with her feet on the bed. The bedroom window had been opened a few inches, and a cardinal was twittering on a branch just beyond the ledge. Both dogs were on the bed next to Dora. Her beloved Freedom's back paws were tangled with Missy's crossed bare feet, and the dog's head was beside Dora's face, the Rottweiler-doberman's smelly breath and lolling tongue inches away. Comfort, the little brown Yorkie, was lying on her thigh, licking her pajama leg.

The dream had been so real. All of her senses had been convinced that she was again fighting that horrific battle. She awoke covered with sweat. *Damn, she needed a shower.*

Missy must have noticed her panicked expression because she climbed onto the bed, and enfolded Dora in her arms. "Shh. It's okay. I've got you. You're with me, baby. It was just a dream. Shh."

Dora's eyes finally focused on Missy's round, smiling, light brown face. Little Comfort maneuvered his way up her body, curling around his own tail on her soft flannel pajama top between her breasts.

"Mmm," Dora said sleepily. "He smells like love."

Missy looked at the little terrier, whose tail end was nearest Dora's face, and raised an eyebrow. "Not too sure that's love you're smelling, babe."

Missy's cellphone rang. She dug into her pants pocket, looked to see who was calling, and answered. "Hey." She paused. "Oh, boy. Well, are the papers important? Can you take them away?" She listened again and finally sat up, her feet on the floor. "All that matters is that he's safe and isn't endangering anyone. No, that's all right. I understand. I'm always here. Call whenever."

She hung up and looked at Dora. "Be glad you don't have family."

"Why? Who was that?"

"My sister, Bai. My father was out wandering the streets again. They're having trouble keeping him in the house. And he does this thing now where he'll take any papers that are lying around, and tear them into little bits. He did that with some bills and paperwork for the business."

Dora was concerned. "How can he run the business?" Missy's father owned and lived for his freight forwarding business, which was not far from Kennedy Airport, and which he had built from scratch as a young man.

"He thinks he can, but that's part of the problem. Bai's husband, Mingzé—we sometimes call him Mike—has been doing most of the work and letting my father think he's doing it. But my father notices and criticizes Mingzé's work and tries to undo it. The whole thing's kind of a mess, actually. Our mother's beside herself."

Dora looked wistful. "Must be nice having family."

Missy gave a faint snort. "Don't kid yourself. This shit's no picnic. I'm basically on call."

Dora's forehead furrowed. "Still, you have people and they care about you and you support each other. I don't have any of that."

Missy gazed steadily back at her. "And if you did—with your family, I mean—you wouldn't be safe. Right?"

"Right, but I don't want my family. I want yours."

Missy gave a little laugh.

Dora blinked. The skin around her eyes tightened and her mouth clenched. "I'm not getting enough sleep," she said, her voice groggy.

"So, go back to sleep. You don't have to be anywhere."

"But the nightmares are crazy. I wake up in the middle of the night with these—they feel like heart attacks!"

"They're panic attacks. I know they feel awful, but they're not dangerous."

The trauma of Dora's battle with the enforcer had lit a fire under much older trauma.

Both Dora and Missy had good medical insurance that included mental health coverage paid for by their employer, Adam Geller of

Geller Investigations. After searching online for a doctor, then vetting her via reviews and a check of her medical credentials, Missy was able to make an appointment for later that day. Several hours later, she drove Dora to the doctor's office. The doctor prescribed a second antidepressant, this one for sleep, and a mood stabilizer. Dora was resistant to taking medication for her anxiety, but Missy patiently explained that she had a medical condition that likely required treatment if she wanted its symptoms to subside. Dora ultimately agreed to take the medication which, she had been told, might take a week, perhaps longer, to have full effect.

• • •

On the following Thursday, Dora and Missy were at their twin desks in the back of the Geller Investigations strip mall storefront. Thelma, the austere, middle-aged office manager, worked the phones and greeted clients in the front, which served as a lobby. Dora looked up as Thelma appeared in the doorway accompanied by a large woman with precisely trimmed eyebrows, simple yet tasteful makeup, and long silver hair that was pulled back in a ponytail held in place by a red scrunchy.

"This is Katie Drucker," Thelma said.

The woman smiled slightly and took a small step into the room. Missy stood and ushered her to a chair that was adjacent to her desk while Dora watched from behind hers.

"Have a seat, Ms. Drucker."

"Katie, please."

"Hi, Katie. I'm Missy Winters and that's Dora Ellison."

The woman nodded. "You're investigators?"

She nodded. "Why don't you tell us why you're here and how we can help."

"I'm here because"—her face reddened and she began to cry,—"because someone murdered my husband."

"I'm so sorry," Missy said. Dora watched and listened but said nothing. Missy continued. "Have you been to the police?"

"Oh, yes. They're investigating. Or, they say they are." The woman rummaged around in her pocketbook, pulled out a few tissues, and wiped her eyes and nose. "But they're getting nowhere that I can see."

Missy said, "Why don't you tell us what happened, in your own words."

Katie looked away and shook her head. She looked embarrassed. "I don't know what happened. He went to the drugstore a week ago today."

"At what time?" Missy asked.

"Eight-thirty at night. The drugstore's open late on weeknights—'til midnight—but we go to sleep by nine-thirty because we have to get up by six to take the dog out."

Missy gave an encouraging nod.

"He didn't come home, so after an hour I went looking for him and when I got to the parking lot it was filled with cops and EMS, and he was—" She began to cry again, sobbing into a tissue. "Sorry," she managed to say.

Missy waited.

Katie sniffled a few times and reached back to thread her ponytail between a thumb and forefinger. She blinked. "He was shot—in the face." She hiccuped twice and began to silently cry again, her shoulders shaking.

Missy paused, her eyes wandering as she digested the information. "What was he doing immediately before going to the drugstore?"

"Watching a murder mystery, of all things." Katie shook her head and swiped her nose with the balled-up tissue. Missy pulled two more tissues from a box on her desk and handed them to Katie.

"Thank you," she said. "I told the police everything I could. They asked if he had enemies or some kind of run-in with someone recently. The answers are no and no."

"Okay," Missy said, thinking. "What are your family relationships like?"

The woman gave a little shrug, raising an eyebrow. "They're reasonably okay. Not perfect, but nothing that would—" She began blinking back tears. "We have kids—we get along. We have grandkids. They're little and"—she smiled—"they light up our lives." Her face crumpled again; she looked helplessly at Missy and managed to pull herself together. "Ray was getting ready to retire, and I'm retired—I was in retail. He had a modest pension and we'd have social security soon, so our family life is, was, in good shape—or so we thought."

"What does—did your husband do for a living?"

"Well, it'll take a minute to tell you." She tightened her lips, focusing. "Until a year and a half ago, he was a filing clerk for the Department of Public Works at county. I worked at a clothing store"—she smiled in Dora's direction—"for us big girls, at the mall." She turned back to Missy. "Anyway, Ray always drank a bit—it wasn't an issue for him, or me for that matter. What do I care? But it was for the county." She bit the inside of a cheek. "He got fired for drinking on his lunch break. But he always was a doer, so after he lost his job he bought a gun shop that had once been a sporting goods store. He—we—bought it at auction, as the previous owner had been in some trouble and needed to give it up. Used to belong to one Tom Bannion. Anyway, lots of sporting goods are bought over the internet nowadays, and the store'd been going downhill, but guns—there's always a market for guns—so the previous owner, this Bannion guy, turned it into a gun shop, and it was popular. It'd been shut down recently due to Bannion's legal troubles, and as soon as we took over, people started coming in. It's attached to a range, which is even more popular than the store." She grinned. "Folks love their guns."

Missy had begun typing notes into her computer. She paused and looked up. "You said we."

"Sorry?"

"You said, 'as soon as we took over.'"

Katie nodded. "Right. I work there part-time, so it's been the two of us."

Missy sat back, tapping the edge of the table with a finger. "What about customers? Were there any disagreements at the business?"

Katie thought about this. "A few, yes. The police asked about that as well. I gave them a few names. I'll give them to you too."

"Good. Do you know if the police have information from anyone who happened to be pulling into or out of the drugstore lot around the time of the shooting, or going into or out of the store?"

Katie shook her head. "Nothing I'm aware of, but they may have information that they're not sharing with me. That's one of the frustrations that brought me to you."

Chapter 2

I'd been thinking about what happened all those years ago—thinking, dwelling, stewing. I did this for years, and the years were well spent. At first, I was too shattered to think. I was physically broken—ruined really. Most days, it was all I could do to drag myself out of bed, and some days I couldn't even do that. I couldn't look in a mirror for weeks—at all. I was deeply hurt, wounded—like an animal—and deeply depressed. When something like this happens, you become less than a human being—not even an animal. A rock or a piece of wood. It's all you can do to survive. And for a long, long time, that's all I did. Survive. Barely.

Once I was able to get myself out of bed, I ate, I sat in a chair, I used the bathroom—and that's about it. I would just sit in a chair for hours and hours. Sleep was just about impossible, and even when I did sleep, the nightmares were unbearable. I saw faces, and I relived what happened, and it was even worse in the dreams.

For a time, I wanted to die. Everything hurt, so why go on? But I had a few people who cared, who encouraged me to live, to survive, to wait. I would get better, they promised, though they didn't say when.

And I did get better. Music helped. I listened to music. I escaped with music. I came alive with music. Music wouldn't hurt me. Wouldn't betray me.

And my people saw the change. They wanted to help. And they did.

Eventually, very slowly, I came to. I woke up. I set about living, if it could be called that. I got into a kind of rhythm. Wake up, eat, do some work, and do my best to act in a reasonably normal way around the people who cared. Try to sleep—take enough sleep meds to get at least the minimum of sleep I could live on.

Do it again. And again.

I did that for a while—quite a while. And eventually, I began to have an idea. The more I thought about the idea, the more I liked it—and the more the idea began to develop. To take shape. To become a plan.

Revenge.

• • •

The next night, before leaving work, Missy said to Dora, "Let's do Shabbat tonight. We can pick up challah and wine on the way home, and we have candles."

Dora looked at her in surprise. "Really?" Dora was Jewish and somewhat observant, whereas Missy had her own personal brand of Buddhism centered around the work of the recently deceased Vietnamese monk Thich Nhat Hanh and the Dali Llama. While she was tolerant of Dora's beliefs, she had never expressed interest in active participation.

"I would love that!" Dora continued.

"Spirituality is healing," Missy said, holding Dora's gaze. "God is healing."

"God? This is quite the day for firsts. I've never heard you talk about God."

Missy grinned with a hint of mischief. "Just because I don't talk about God doesn't mean I don't believe in God. Buddhism is all about direct experience, and I honor yours—which includes your connection to God." She rose from her desk and walked over to Dora, who was seated at her own desk, and cradled her head against her chest.

"No public displays of affection in the workplace!" Thelma was in the doorway, shaking her finger and bellowing at a far greater volume than was needed.

Dora tried to push Missy away, but Missy held Dora's head tightly against her. She spoke to the office manager. "Just because you aren't in love, doesn't mean we can't show ours."

Thelma glared back and her lips and the skin around her eyes tightened. A hint of tears shone in her eyes.

"Sorry, Thelma," Missy said, with a hint of contrition. "Maybe I shouldn't have said that."

"I don't know what you mean," Thelma said, dismissively. "Doesn't matter to me what you say or do, really." She turned and disappeared toward the front of the office.

They stopped at the supermarket and bought the supplies they had discussed along with a sweet, moist *babka* for dessert. They said the three prayers, the first over the candles, welcoming the peace of Shabbat as a lover welcomes his or her bride. The second prayer was the blessing of the fruit of the vine, the *borei pri hagafen.* The third prayer was the *hamotzi,* the blessing over the bread, which was a fresh challah.

"When we do this," Dora commented, "it feels like we have our own little family."

Missy smiled and widened her eyes in agreement.

Both dogs knew from the sound of the prayers and the smell of roasting chicken that they would soon be receiving bits of moist, savory Shabbat challah.

Dora and Missy enjoyed their roasted chicken with baked potatoes and spinach, followed by delicious chocolate *babka.*

As they finished their feast, Dora asked Missy, "Do you really want to go to temple services with me?"

Missy nodded slowly and thoughtfully. "I think it'll help you heal. Saying the prayers, seeing the rabbi, and hearing our beautiful cantor sing—it'll give you strength."

As they got in the car, Missy's cellphone rang. She looked to see who was calling and said, "It's my sister. I have to take this."

Dora didn't say anything, but drove on, doing her best to enjoy the cool, clear evening and the newly blooming dogwood and cherry trees along the sidewalks between their apartment and the synagogue.

Missy listened and said, "oh" every now and then. After ending the call, Missy was quiet as they pulled into a spot in front of the synagogue. Finally, she said, "My father was helping cook dinner tonight."

"That sounds like a good thing," Dora offered.

"He brought a jar outside, filled it with dirt, and poured it into the pot with the food, just as my mother was about to serve." Missy was blinking rapidly, holding back tears.

"Wow," Dora said.

"They want me to come and see him, so we can all talk about what to do."

Dora pressed her lips together and didn't answer. Finally, she nodded toward the front of the synagogue, where a crowd had gathered. She got out of the car, and Missy followed. People were in the little memorial garden, standing on the bricks that had been engraved with the names of donors in memory of family and loved ones who had been murdered in the Holocaust.

Covering much of the front eastern wall of the synagogue were words painted in white: "Death To Jews," and a second phrase, "Long Live Hitler." Beneath the two phrases, a large, white swastika had been painted.

Missy clutched Dora's arm with both hands. Dora turned to her with a purposeful look. "You were right. Coming to synagogue did give me strength."

• • •

The two women returned to their apartment following the rabbi's service, which was adjusted on the fly to address the antisemitic desecration of the synagogue and the increasing trend toward antisemitism in society. Missy went immediately to her computer, while Dora riffled around in the fridge, cracked open a beer, and then poured a glass of white wine for Missy.

"Thanks, babe," Missy said, glancing away from the computer long enough to take the glass from Dora. "Incredible how many kinds of anti-semitism there are now, and how some of the most popular talking heads on the news are having their proponents on as guests and cosigning their bullshit."

Dora took a swig of her beer and nodded. "Maybe we oughta drive to D.C. or wherever they are and take a few out to the woodshed." She was trying hard to keep her rage in check. While the anger was refreshing and helped her emerge from the emotional cocoon she'd wrapped herself in following her battle with Moran, she was finding her rage at the synagogue's desecration overwhelming and intrusive.

Missy laughed. "I see you're starting to feel better."

Dora had been smiling an empty smile for Missy's sake, but now even that smile faded. "Nah, I don't know. But I do have an idea of something that might help."

"First, let me tell you what I'm seeing here. It's crazy!"

"Okay."

Missy sat back and looked at the screen. "So, we've got QAnon—we already know about them." She sipped her wine.

Dora raised her beer in a mock toast. "QAnon—great source of information, America." She shook her head. "How is it possible anyone but meth heads with third grade educations believes them?"

Missy gave a hum of agreement. "Tells you something." She read on. "Then you've got Ye—Kanye West, who talks more bullshit about Jews."

"Lovely," Dora agreed.

"Who a lot of people believe." Missy turned to her. "Says here that as recently as 1938, 60 percent of the American population believed the stereotype of Jews as greedy, sniveling international conspiracists."

Dora shrugged. "I'm not surprised."

Missy nodded sadly, then thought of something. "What was it you said you wanted to do—you said you needed to do something that would make you feel better. What was it—play with the dogs, maybe?"

"Well, that too," Dora said, finishing the last of her beer. "What I meant—what I need to do is … fight. As in punch someone in the face."

• • •

Once I decided I would seek justice, or rather revenge—I liked that word better—I knew I would have to plan, and plan carefully. I wasn't dealing with idiots. I was dealing with people who had some intelligence—who had been around the block, even if they really were garbage, when it came right down to it. They had businesses, wives, families. I couldn't just storm in and start shooting.

How would I approach this problem; it was more than a problem really—it was a necessity. It was my life. How would I right all that they had made wrong all those years ago?

Slowly, for one. Very, very slowly. I really didn't know what I was doing, at first. I started slowly and with lots and lots of caution. That was my plan at the very beginning. I took ten years to do the first one, then another five for the second. But after that, I gained some confidence.

But back to my plan. To start with, I didn't have a gun. But I did know where to get one, and what I needed was an untraceable gun.

Now, did I need a different gun for each of the killings? I thought about this for quite some time and I came to the conclusion that no, I didn't think so. I could use the same gun. I was pretty sure that there was a way for the cops to figure out it was used for more than one murder—something to do with ballistics—but so what? Who cares? Where did that get the cops? My gun would be unregistered and there'd be no way to trace it to me. Who the hell was I? I had no record. I was nobody, as far as the police were concerned—a law-abiding goddamned citizen. So I made sure to give the police nothing to grab onto.

• • •

Dora went into the bedroom and stripped off her clothes in favor of black sweatpants, a sports bra, and a magenta T-shirt sporting black lettering that read: "Shay's MMA." After kissing Missy, she threw on a sweatshirt and took the elevator to the ground floor and went out to the parking lot to her Subaru WRX Turbo.

She smiled at the early spring lavender that bloomed along one side of the parking lot. This was her favorite time of year, a time of birth and rebirth, when what was destroyed or gone was replaced with hope and renewal. Her parking spot was in the rear of the lot, behind which a honeysuckle shrub had sprouted climbing tentacle vines. She went to the plant and buried her face in the riot of yellow and white flowers. She pulled one of the blooms from the vine and squeezed its base between her fingers, pulling on the stem until a droplet of nectar formed at the base of the flower. She licked the droplet, savored its sweet taste, and smiled all the way to Shay's.

Shay herself, dark-eyed, and with an expression that was half grin half grimace, was seated on a stool at the counter just inside the front door to the gym, her eyes on a computer screen. She looked up as Dora entered, and her black eyes crinkled with delight. "Hey!"

Dora asked, "Okay if I work out?"

Shay nodded toward two women who were working out on the mat. "Why not?"

Dora knew both women. Their gym nicknames were Whale and Flex. Both wore full pads on their elbows, knees, midsections, and feet, as well as gloves and headgear. They were transitioning from standing and striking to grappling on the ground and back again.

Three other women, nicknamed Axe, Bottoms, and someone Dora didn't recognize, watched from the sidelines, where they sat on the mat shouting encouragement or friendly derision.

"Hey," Dora called out.

The women nodded and greeted her, but remained focused on the combatants.

Whale was over six feet tall and weighed well over two hundred pounds. She was primarily a striker, though, and like all of the women, she was well-versed in a variety of combat techniques and styles.

Whale was known for her power. She was the foremost knockout striker at the gym by virtue of her size, strength, and technique. Here, among training partners, Whale kept her power in check … to a degree.

Flex was a submission specialist—adept at crafting holds and submissions of all kinds from any position or circumstance, including a standing position. She loved using knees and elbows from the standing clinch position. She was expert at using her opponents' power against them and was quick to "take their backs," so as to "sink in her hooks" and snake her forearm under the opponents' chin so as to choke them out or "put them to sleep." She differed from other submission specialists, including Bottoms, who was seated further along the wall, watching. Bottoms preferred to seek submissions from the bottom position, with the opponent on top of her—a rarity in mixed martial arts, or "MMA."

When Dora's turn came, she was paired with Axe, a lithe blonde woman who was slightly taller than Dora at five foot nine, but at least ten pounds lighter, with straw-colored hair and a pink, flushed complexion.

Dora had never sparred with Axe, so she did not know what to expect. She quickly found out. Using some kind of footwork deception, Axe slid forward and kicked Dora in the stomach with a front leg roundhouse kick, instantly re-chambered and kicked at the right side of Dora's head. The first kick landed low on Dora's chest pad, though Dora was able to slip the kick slightly by sliding back with it. She blocked the second kick with her left forearm, grabbed Axe's ankle, and lifted Axe's leg while walking toward her, forcing Axe to hop backward several steps. Dora then kicked Axe's plant leg out from under her and Axe crashed to the ground. Dora landed in side control, took full mount, and began raining gym versions of ground-and-pound on Axe's head.

"Can I go?" Another woman, this one also long and lean, with a tight Afro and walnut-colored skin, waved a hand.

"Sure, Long." Shay nodded from the front desk, then walked to the mat, bowed, and took a seat at the edge to watch.

Long bowed to Dora, and put out her hand. "Fahira Long."

Dora took her hand and bowed in return. "Dora Ellison."

Long stepped back as Shay said, "Fight," then flicked out an impossibly quick jab that sliced Dora's cheek like a paper cut. Before Dora could react, she hit Dora with a three-punch combination—a jab, cross, hook—which rocked her. The woman used her length to generate power that began in her legs and ended on Dora's face.

Three more punches landed, this time to Dora's body. Long slid back just in time to avoid Dora's takedown dive. The woman sprawled and Dora found her head in a guillotine choke, the woman's bony forearm deep below Dora's chin and squeezing her throat.

She didn't want to, but Dora made the quick decision to cheat rather than submit. She pinched a bit of skin on Long's forearm and would have pinched off the fingerful of skin entirely if Long hadn't released her hold. She sat back, breathing heavily, a hurt look on her face. "What's up with that?" Long demanded.

Dora looked surprised and feigned ignorance. "What's up with what?"

"Oh, I get it." Long nodded slowly. "And I'll remember."

Dora looked at Shay, who was smiling slightly. "Where'd you get *her*?" Dora asked, laughing.

Shay laughed. "She's an instructor. Brad DeRico, a guy I know from the city, recommended her. She's something. She can do just about everything."

"And I don't cheat." Long was looking at Dora steadily.

Dora looked back at her. "Well, good for you," Dora replied.

Chapter 3

Why wait five years before killing another? I was so careful, and that took time, of course—maybe too much time. And there was the fear after that first one—fear of being caught. Fear that someone recognized me.

But the biggest reason I had to wait five more years after killing the first one, was that I had to drink a pint of brandy to do it. As soon as I drove away, I had to pull over to the side of the road to puke. Every time I tried to think about going after them I'd get to shaking and sweating so bad I had to stop and watch TV or lose myself in doing something else, to just get back to normal again.

Then there were the nightmares and the flashbacks. I'd wake up and think it happened again. Or I'd be somewhere and think I saw one of them and I'd feel my lunch start to come up, and then I'd get that bitter bile in the back of my throat and I'd swallow and swallow, but that bitterness would still be there.

On top of all that, the trauma took five years to fade even a little bit —at least enough to stop being paralyzed. To get my shit together enough to do something, and I had a bunch of help getting there.

It was worth it. The first one went just fine. And it was so rewarding. And now, the second had gone just as well—and was even more rewarding. Maybe the long wait wasn't necessary. I know I'm careful; I was careful before, I'll be careful next time. But five years just isn't necessary. I could be dead before I'm done, and that wouldn't do. And now that two are gone, I'm eager for number three. Really eager. So, who's going to be next? Who's going to be number three?

• • •

Greg Walker was sitting at his dining room table, finishing his morning oatmeal. He took his oatmeal with a splash of milk and a sprinkling of crushed graham crackers. He was eyeing the box of candy he had bought for his wife and would give to her after she got home that evening. He forced his eyes away. He craved sweets anytime he was nervous, and he was nervous now.

If he opened that box and ate any of the candy, Sue would have a fit. The woman couldn't have cared less about a candlelit dinner or a string of pearls, but she loved her candy. Valentine's Day, her birthday, Mother's Day—candy went with just about everything—even on any old day like today. She especially loved those heart-shaped boxes, which added her idea of romance to the proceedings. And if the candy had a second level—if, after finishing the last piece, you lifted the paper and there was more! Woohoo! Now that was her idea of Christmas! But you didn't see that so much anymore. He sighed. So much wasn't what it used to be.

Buying candy for his wife gave him a faint hope that their marriage, which had come to seem routine and perfunctory in recent years, might see some life. The hope was barely there, hence his focus on the candy, rather than the marriage.

While he ate, he thought about what he would do today. He had work, but much of his computer networking business was entirely on-line; he had set it up that way, and it suited him fine. Now and then he had to visit clients, which wasn't so bad, as long as he was working on their networks. He much preferred that to meeting with the clients, who were bound to have all sorts of expectations—about his work, the time frame, the cost. He had little patience for their dissatisfaction. Much better to work from home and send them a bill.

But he had little work today. He followed a spoonful of oatmeal with a sip of coffee and glanced out the window. The sun was shining, and the temperature, according to his watch, was a balmy sixty-five degrees. He could work on his garden; he had to put down another layer of soil, plant his spring vegetables, and spread mulch around them.

Or, he could get another tattoo. He was filling up his second sleeve with designs that were usually suggested by Cindy, his tattoo artist. So far, she had woven in images of panthers and owls—symbolizing courage and wisdom—along with abstract designs, all of which he thought were terrific. He had to admit he was partial to tribal art, but he didn't want to be associated with any actual tribes, so he'd rejected that idea. Too bad—but Cindy had plenty of other designs to choose from.

He decided he would break up the day, head over to the garden store, work in the yard for a while, then do a bit of business work and follow that up with a visit to the Club for a few drinks and perhaps shoot a little pool. After the Club, he would cook dinner for himself, Sue, and Theo— if his son was around.

He wondered if a Yankees spring training game might be on tonight. Spring training had just begun. He followed the Yankees and the football Giants as obsessively as he did everything else. He filled every day with as much activity as he could think of, and then filled himself up with a few beers, a few vodka tonics or vodka with cranberry, and then a few more straight vodkas. That was often enough to keep his anxiety and OCD at bay.

He was usually able to distract himself from his thoughts, his memories, his awarenesses, and ultimately, his consciousness. Pouring alcohol over the whole mix seemed to help.

At the end of the day, he often ended up at the Club, where he would do his heaviest drinking. That he had to drive home didn't matter. He was expert at driving drunk—even in blackouts, which were all too common and growing more so. But he always got home, and he was never stopped.

It was his superpower.

All of that—the constant activity, followed by the incessant drinking—was just part of Greg's focus. Or, more accurately, his intent not to focus. The other part—the dangerous part—was, instead of running from his memories, his bad dreams, his thoughts—on the most dangerous days, he ran toward them.

· · ·

Dora was seated, cross-legged, on the floor of their apartment next to the living room coffee table, working on a puzzle. Freedom lay with her chin on Dora's thigh. Missy's head rested on the cushioned arm of the couch as she read the newspaper on her iPad, one leg bent beneath her and the other crossed over it.

At a glance, Dora's puzzle looked all but impossible. The image was of a desert—all sand and very nearly one color. Dora loved the challenge of scouring for subtle patterns made, in this case, by faded footprints or wind-blown sand. Such subtleties could be matched to one another if one looked carefully enough. Her approach to puzzles was similar to her approach to criminal investigations: look closely and identify the patterns.

Missy turned to Dora, her expression stricken. "The *Chronicle* has an article about the vandalism at the synagogue. They cite statistics showing there's more and more of this—not just here, but pretty much everywhere."

Dora didn't answer right away. She was letting the information sink in. Her inner response was the beginning of a quiet rage—like a simmering kettle on the verge of boiling.

"Not surprised," was all she said.

"Are we still going to Charlie and Christine's this afternoon?" Missy asked.

"Oh, I forgot all about that. What time are we supposed to be there?"

"They said two, but … whenever."

Dora nodded slowly. "Let's drive past the synagogue on the way. I want to see it again." She navigated puzzles by looking at the pieces, often while doing something else, and the patterns began to resolve in her subconscious. Then she could start to fit them together, and the process continued, at an ever-deepening level.

She had been stroking the bristly top of Freedom's head while the big dog snored blissfully, her eyes closed. Comfort lay curled on the floor nearest where Missy sat on the couch.

Dora took her phone from her pocket and dialed their new client. "Ms. Drucker? It's Dora Ellison, from Geller Investigations."

"Call me Katie, please."

"Hi, Katie. I wanted to go over a few things. You said that … what happened … was over at the drugstore on Park and Evergreen?"

"That's right. In the parking lot."

"And what did you say he was picking up?"

"I don't believe I said. Is that important?"

"It could be."

"He was picking up blood pressure medication."

"Was there anything else?"

She sighed and suddenly sounded tearful, and Dora realized that her call might be forcing the woman to face feelings she might be avoiding. "Something for my migraines. I get them a lot." Her tone was suddenly testy. "I'm getting one now."

"And that's it?"

"Well, I guess I can tell you. Ray took antidepressants … when he took them." Katie was back to teary again.

Dora was silent a moment. "Did he go off them a lot?"

"Now and then."

"How was he when he didn't take them?"

"Angry and … and sometimes sad. Anxious."

"Angry, like how?"

"He yelled. Hit the table with his fist. When he missed a dose, he had a shorter fuse, but behind that, I think he was anxious. Can we get off this subject?"

"I'll see about getting hold of any surveillance video the drugstore has. Can you tell me a little more about Ray?"

"Like what?" She sounded defensive, and Dora wondered if the questions about medication had put the woman off.

"What was he like in a more general sense?"

"You mean when he was on his meds? He was a good guy. Didn't always remember things—like our anniversary. But on the whole, he was a decent husband."

"What did you like to do together?"

"We tried to find TV shows we could watch together. We did that a few days a week. We did other things separately—watched separate shows. I went shopping—for food and clothes. He was into cars, and he shopped—not to buy, but to look. He was into cars since he was a teenager."

"Did you socialize with other couples?"

She hesitated. "Not very often. We didn't know a lot of couples. We both had friends—but they were two separate groups, his friends and mine."

"Tell me about Ray's friends?" Dora asked.

She didn't answer right away. Then she said, "Actually, now that I think of it, he didn't really have very many."

"He didn't have many friends?"

"Well, he went to this place—he called it the Club."

"The Club?"

"The John Farmer Country Club. It was originally known as the Tanberry Country Club after the upscale section of the north shore in which it is located."

"Oh, yeah. I know it. He went there a lot?"

"Not so much in recent years. Was there all the time until oh, about seven years ago. Had a couple of good—well, I wouldn't call them good —but they were friends he hung out with there. Three, especially. Wayne, Keith, and Greg. He was busy with the range and the store, which got busier and busier since Covid died down, so he just didn't have time to go there anymore, far as I know. But he used to be there all the time."

"Wayne, Keith, and Greg. The John Farmer Club. Do these guys have last names? And phone numbers, if you can get them."

"Hmm," she said. "I'll have to get back to you on that." She returned to her earlier thoughts. "Ray was not the easiest guy. He had a temper and people thought he was sort of nasty, but he was really just sensitive and anxious. Easily upset."

"Thin-skinned?" Dora suggested.

"You could say. I loved him—I still do. I just think he was easily hurt. I guess that's another way of saying it. People found him too intense."

Dora's eyes wandered around the room, paused on Missy, and descended to Comfort. "You said your husband had been fired from a previous job—something related to drinking. Can you tell me more about that? Did he talk about it? Was he angry about it?"

"Yeah, he was—for a while. Losing his job that way affected his pension. He still got it, but it was less than it might have been—and we rely on that pension—but it's less of a worry now that the range and the shop are doing well. But he was definitely unhappy about it."

"Did he blame the person who fired him?"

"To some extent, I think he did."

"Was there a lot of conflict around the situation at that time? Did he lash out at the person?"

"He thought it was unfair. He understood he screwed up, but he thought losing his job was overkill. He didn't hurt anyone. He didn't drink all that much, but he did get into it with his boss at the time—a guy named Earl Lincoln."

"What can you tell me about him?"

"Not much. He was Raymond's boss at the county, and he was a bit of a prick. That's how Raymond talked about him—a bit of a prick."

"Tell me about the conflict."

"There isn't much to tell. All I know is the guy smelled liquor on him and fired him. So, Raymond gave the guy a piece of his mind—told him how much getting fired was going to screw up his family, his kids, his future."

"Any idea where I can find Earl Lincoln?"

"Probably the county Department of Public Works' office."

"What about the conflicts at the gun range and the shop?"

"We were thinking of opening a restaurant bar attached to the shop and range."

"Really? You can have a bar attached to a shooting range?"

"I know it might sound weird, but any drinking would have to come after people use the range, never before. Our rule would have been anyone who'd had a drink within 24 hours wouldn't be allowed to shoot. You wouldn't be allowed to go from the bar to the range. We had a system to oversee that."

"And how'd it go?"

"We never got that far. It was just an idea we were putting together."

"So, where was the conflict?"

"We got the idea from a group of customers who always came in together. They were gun enthusiasts, as Raymond was. Nothing wrong with that."

"Nope."

"And they did like to drink. Anyway, they got to talking about it one time, and they brought the idea to Ray, who thought it had some merit.

So, we looked into it and were just figuring out how to go about it, when he … you know."

"The conflict?"

"Those guys were pretty raucous. Nothing to do with the bar and gun range idea, but they were loud and disturbed a few of our other regulars, and they got into it—the two groups. Ray had to separate them. Apparently, the two groups didn't like each other, and the other group—not the guys with the gun idea, but the others—got pretty bent out of shape about it."

"Do you have the names of anyone in either—preferably both—of these groups?"

"Sorry. No." Her tone brightened. "There's something else. Ray bought a 'Vette about a year ago, and he had a big fight with the guy who sold it to him."

"About what?"

"Price—the fight was after he bought it. The guy came back to him and tried to basically extort more money. He said there was some part that he didn't realize was much more expensive than Ray paid for. It was a huge fight, and I didn't understand it because they'd made a deal, and the guy wanted to go back on it. You don't have the right to come back afterward and say, 'Hey, wait a minute, I should have charged you more.'"

"So he wanted more money after the sale was complete? What kind of part was it?"

"Some kind of shock absorber. Give me a sec—let me think. A double adjustable shock. That was it—a double adjustable canister shock. Said it was six grand and the car was a '69 'Vette."

"Do you remember who this guy was?"

"Oh, yeah. Dennis McCrae. He's known as the 'Vette Man. Listed online that way. Works out of the gas station and repair shop at the corner of Laurel and Park."

"Isn't that McCrae Brothers Repair?"

"That's the one!"

Chapter 4

I knew I needed help killing these assholes—help from people I could trust, and I had a few of those. People who could keep a secret. Two came to mind, and I thought long and hard before I told them what I wanted to do. After all, I was planning to murder people so I'd better be damned sure the people I told would be trustworthy.

Well, I finally told them. They knew what had happened to me. They knew how I had suffered. They knew I was devastated and was lucky I didn't just take myself out. They knew how hard it was for me to cope, how hard it was for me to live—to get through each day. It was like climbing a mountain every single day of the week.

And they knew I was angry. Really, deeply angry. And they were angry too. I knew that before I told them. What I didn't know was how they would react to being a party to killing people. That would make them criminals too. Accessories.

So, one night we all had dinner, and after a couple of drinks, I sucked it up and I told them. And I kind of held my breath as I waited for their reactions.

Well, they looked at each other—and I could see they were thinking about how serious this was. What I was asking was no joke. I don't think I was worried that they'd turn me in just for talking about it. It was just a conversation, and I'm not sure a conversation about murder is a crime. Maybe it is—I don't know. But I could see they were looking at each other, and there was this unspoken communication going on about whether they should do this with me. Maybe they were thinking they could get out of there right then—I probably would be.

But that's not what happened; they surprised me. I was pretty sure that one of them would do it because of who he was in my life. We were close. We'd always been close. I was pretty sure that the threat of the law, of jail, would not come between us—and it didn't. He was cool. He said, "Absolutely—I'm in." And that felt good. Really, damned good.

I had an idea that the other person would go along too, if the first person did, so I made sure to ask them in the right order.

Which worked out just fine. The first one said yes because of the nature of our relationship; the second said yes because the first person did.

Now, we had to figure out how to set about killing these people without getting caught.

• • •

Dora walked into Evergreen Drugs while Missy took a phone call outside. Several minutes later, she entered the store and found Dora waiting.

"My father is calling Mingzé by my grandfather's first name," Missy said. She looked frightened. "We're trying to figure out a day and time we can all get together and have my father there, so we can figure out what to do."

Dora didn't know what to say, so she led Missy to the consultation counter, where they were met by a young green-eyed woman with blonde and purple streaked hair that was parted on one side.

The girl smiled. "How can I help you?"

Dora spoke in a low voice. "I'm investigating the murder that occurred in your parking lot a few days ago."

The girl's eyes nervously darted away from Dora to areas behind and around her.

Dora continued. "I work for Geller Investigations. I'm here to see the footage from the surveillance cameras that cover the lot."

The girl glanced to her left. "You'll have to speak with the manager. Could you step over here?" She stepped to the empty counter spot to her left and spoke softly to a man with silver-framed glasses, dark beige skin, and a fringe of gray hair behind a receding hairline. He wore a green apron emblazoned with the drugstore's logo. He stepped to the counter in front of Dora.

"How can I help you?" he asked.

"As I mentioned to …" Dora nodded toward the counter she'd just left, "we're investigating the murder that occurred in your parking lot a few days ago and would like to see the security footage."

The man, whose bronze badge said his name was Saul, looked surprised. "The police were already here and viewed the video."

Missy took a small, thin case from a side pants pocket and proffered a business card. "We're with Geller Investigations. Our office is just a block and a half west of here, in the strip mall. We've solved several local murders in the last couple of years. You might have read about us in the *Chronicle*."

Saul smiled. "I believe I have. But showing you our security video—I'm not sure corporate would—"

"You might be helping to solve a murder, Saul," Missy added. "Corporate might love that."

"And would corporate really have to know?" Dora said, in a low, conspiratorial tone. "Unless, of course, you were in the paper as a hero."

Saul's smile widened, and he stepped to a door in the counter and swung it back, allowing the two women access to the back area of the drugstore. "Follow me."

They followed Saul to a small, empty office in which two computers sat on desks. Their screens displayed live images of the aisles and counter areas of the store, along with the parking lot and a small section of the front sidewalk area outside the entrance to the store.

Saul sat down at one of the computers, pressed several keys, moved the mouse, and the black and white image on the screen in front of him changed to a grainy nighttime image. He scrubbed through the video, keeping an eye on the time stamps. He stopped once, glanced again at the time stamp, and began scrubbing through again, much more slowly.

"By the way, the person who committed the murder was not in the store as far as we can tell. Ah, here. This is what you're looking for," he said.

"Here's the victim's car entering the lot." He pointed. "And you can see the victim enter the store."

Dora and Missy watched a lanky 50-ish man with a long face in a lightweight sweater get out of a light-colored Chevy Equinox. He walked toward and beneath the camera and, ostensibly, into the store. No one else was in the frame.

Saul fast-forwarded the tape. "I'm not going to bring up the tape of him in the store, but we have it if you need it."

Dora nodded.

Saul said, "Here he is again, about ten minutes later, exiting the store."

"Could you back it up a bit, please," Dora asked. "I'd like to see if anyone else—a lookout, perhaps—might have left just prior and been waiting for him. And could you show us the view from the register, so we can see if he's followed or watched as he left?"

"Sure." Saul provided the views, then sat back, waiting.

Dora and Missy watched, glancing at one another. "Okay, now let's get back to the lot, as he leaves," Dora requested.

Saul switched the view back to the parking lot, and Dora and Missy watched as a Toyota Prius entered the lot and pulled up next to Drucker's car on the driver's side.

Moments later, Ray Drucker exited the store with a package, walked to his car, opened the door, and got in.

Seconds later, the Prius's driver's side door opened and a hooded figure emerged, walked around the back of the car, and approached Drucker's window, which rolled down. After a pause, the owner of the Prius pulled a handgun from the hoodie's right-side pocket, fired into

Drucker's face, waited a beat, walked back to the Prius, opened the door, got in, and drove away.

Saul sat back, one hand covering his mouth. He paused, composing himself. "Well, there you go," he said.

Missy said, "Could you replay the part starting from where the other car pulls in?"

Saul rewound the tape and played it again.

"See if there's a plate number on the Prius," Dora said.

"The police asked that too," Saul said, freezing the tape after the Prius parked and zooming on its rear license plate. "It's obscured." The plate was indeed obscured.

"Run it again," Dora requested.

"Okay, freeze it there," Missy said, as the driver got out of the car, passed behind it, and was briefly in profile to the camera. "Can you take a screenshot of the guy's face and maybe print it out?"

"I can, but the face is in shadow because of the hoodie. Not sure what you'll get."

"That's okay."

Saul hit a few keys and a screenshot appeared, enlarged, on the screen. He moused to a "Print" menu and moments later a sheet of paper swooshed from a printer.

"Hmm, not great," Dora said. "Okay, run it again, and … stop it there," she said, suddenly, as the Prius's owner was looking at Drucker. "Look at that! Do you have a zoom function? Can you zoom on the guy in the car's face?"

Saul did as he was asked.

"Look at his face," Dora said eagerly to Missy.

"I see what you mean." Missy looked at Dora, who nodded in agreement. "Drucker rolled down his window and smiled," Missy observed. "And the way he smiled—he knows this guy."

• • •

Greg sat at the desk in his home office, in front of several computer screens. One showed diagrams of several clients' network systems that were waiting for parts to be operational. Another gave him access to their networks and allowed him to adjust many of their settings remotely. Several inches from his left hand was a large bag of peanut M&Ms. Near his right hand was a tall vodka tonic over ice with a slice of lime. He had been making changes to the networks, setting up security protocols, creating access for new employees, integrating functionality related to the companies' industries and clients, and checking and double-checking his work—all of which was helped along by copious amounts of sugar and alcohol, which he thought of as indispensable for his work.

The doorbell rang. He had a built-in visceral reaction that told him to leap out of his chair and run out the back door, hop the fence to the neighbor's yard, and keep running; but that was based on activities that were far in his past and fears that had never manifested. *Relax, that's probably the Dorex delivery with my parts.* He listened; perhaps Sue or Theo would answer the door. The bell rang again. He got up and headed for the front door, past Theo, who was wearing headphones and gazing at some video on his phone or playing a game on Steam or one of the other platforms he frequented for much of his waking life. He thought he heard Sue, upstairs, drying her hair.

He opened the door to Johnny, the Dorex delivery guy—tall and thin with deep brown skin and a permanent smile. "What's shakin'?" Johnny asked, rhetorically. Greg and Johnny, whose name was Johnny Ray Jackson, were on friendly speaking terms and often chatted, but Greg was not in the mood to chat today and didn't answer. He signed for the package, took it, turned away, and closed the door. Then he went back to his office, removed the router extenders from their packaging, and briefly examined them. He then put on his coat, went out to the car, and drove over to McCrae's, where he parked next to one of the pumps. He went into the office and found Mateo, scruffy, with tousled reddish hair and a long dark beard, sitting at the desk.

"He's under the first car, Mr. Walker," Mateo said, nodding toward the work area.

Greg stepped to the bay's entrance, then turned back to Mateo. "What do you have in there?" he asked, out of politeness.

"A '67—last of the C2 'Vettes," Mateo answered proudly, then anticipated Greg's next question. "Engine's a four twenty-seven. Four thirty-five horse. I think there's a '54 in the other bay."

"Mmm," Greg said, doing his best to sound impressed. "Listen, I don't want to bother the boss. My wife was in last Tuesday and he said we need new tires. I need the price before she brings the car in."

Mateo nodded and opened a notebook. He ran his thumb down a left page, then the right page, and stopped halfway down. "Here you go. Sue Walker, the 2019 Mustang GT. That would be the AMR gloss black, which would be $575 for the front two, including labor."

"So he said we need the front two?"

Mateo nodded. "Well, you can't do just one, so, yeah."

"Thanks." Greg left the office, returned to his car, filled it with gas, and headed north to the Club.

The Club was situated at the far end of a cul-de-sac, in the center of which was a garden whose flowers encircled a statue of Zeus hurling a thunderbolt. Inside the Club's entrance was a white 400-square-foot foyer with a marble floor that was ringed with Greek statuettes on ornate five-foot stone pillars. On either side of the far end of the foyer, twin dark-stained wooden staircases rose and met above a plaque on which a coat-of-arms was carved with the letters WR in old gothic script. Below the plaque was the doorway to the bar, and beyond the bar was an upscale restaurant.

Greg walked the length of the foyer, his heels tapping the marble floor, and passed through the doorway and into the Club's restaurant bar, where he stood for a moment, surveying the scene in the wood-paneled room.

As usual, the bartender was Bart, with glasses, shaggy brown hair, and matching beard. He grinned at Greg from behind the bar. "Usual?"

Greg nodded.

A white-haired man of about seventy in a blue suit jacket, matching pants, and white shirt with no tie was alone at the far end of the bar, nursing a whiskey on the rocks and dipping his fingers into a plate of candied pecans. Two men in their thirties were at one table—Greg didn't think he'd seen them before.

At another table was a group of men whose ages ranged from mid-twenties to early forties. They were frequent customers and were known, to those who knew them as a group, as the Wires.

Bart said, "There you go," and placed a pint of Guinness and a neat scotch on napkins in front of Greg, who took his drinks to the table next to the one where the Wires were congregated and gazed at the screen of a high-end laptop computer. One of the group, a large unshaven bear of a man with a tangled mop of black hair, a puffy face, and heavy lips, looked at a spot over Greg's left shoulder and grinned.

"Seen the art?"

Greg raised an eyebrow. "Art? As in…?"

"On East Street. Can't miss it." He turned toward the pale young man with light blond hair and blue eyes who was operating the computer. "Cloud. Bring up the art."

Cloud's eyes flicked toward his speaker. "Way ahead of you, PB."

Greg noted the pints of beer in front of each of them, some full, some empty, some in between. Each had a full shot glass of whiskey as well. He could tell by their demeanor and language that these were not their first drinks. He sipped his scotch and chased it with the Guinness.

The Wires were an informal collection of individuals that had long inhabited the Club, with different members over the years, and were in a true sense the Club's *raison d'être*. They were known informally as the Wires, which was an extension of "the Y.R.'s," whose full name was a description that was rarely spoken aloud.

Cloud opened the video, and Greg watched the "artwork" progress on the front of the local synagogue. When the video ended, he merely nodded—a carefully tamped-down affirmation.

The Wires, or Y.R.'s, at the Club all led normal, even boring lives, and lived for their secret identities as anonymous rock stars in their universe—fomenting and exuberantly supporting others like themselves online and in secret gatherings—as had generations before them, many of them based at the John Farmer Club.

Polar Bear, or PB, was Bruce Jameson, who worked at a nearby Chicken-4U as a day manager. Behind the computer was Lawrence Tilden, aka Cloud or White Cloud, a computer programmer at a New York hedge fund. Next to Bruce was Chris Lombardo, aka Cream Cheese, who was stocky and of medium height, with a pasty face, a crew cut, and enormous dark eyes. He had played football at a major midwestern university, where he had also enjoyed a partial sports scholarship and the perks that came along with it—many of them involving his team's female fans, willing or not. He was now a personal trainer at a local gym.

Greg took another swallow of scotch, then a pull at his Guinness. "I understand you boys've got some big days coming up."

All four except PB looked up at him eagerly. PB never looked directly at anyone.

"Got that right," said Cream Cheese. "Lampoon Day in two weeks."

Greg allowed himself a faint smile. You never wanted to look too enthusiastic about anything with these guys. Enthusiasm implied weakness. Vulnerability. He was about to ask what they had planned for these events, making sure to restrain any indication that he cared too much, but his phone buzzed—a text. He took it out and froze.

"Problem?" Cream Cheese said, raising a derisive eyebrow.

Greg allowed his eyes to flicker in his direction. "Nothing I can't handle."

"Prob'ly his wife telling him to wash the dishes," Cloud remarked.

"Whupped," PB muttered, shaking his head.

Greg cast them both a faintly contemptuous glance. "Least there are women who would marry me," he said, and everyone laughed. He turned to White Cloud. "And hey, Fluffy … we can afford a dishwasher." More laughter. He spoke their language, which was one of casual slang and implied dominance. He drained his scotch and chased it with Guinness, then stepped to the bar and slid the scotch glass toward Bart. "Double." He looked again at the text and felt the cold sweat break out on his cheeks, chest, and arms.

Someone had murdered Ray Drucker.

He had only this morning been thinking about his old friends, who had been such a major part of his life at this very club. Back in the day, they'd been pillars of the Club. But he never thought of them anymore. They'd been out of touch for years—and that's the way he liked it.

Perhaps he'd dreamt of them, as he often did—of what had happened—of what they'd done. Of being chased. Of the casual brutality, of the violence—and of trouble spiraling in from all directions. And all of it so much more than they'd bargained for.

They'd managed to escape by going their separate ways. He'd thought he was safe—that they all were.

But the trouble had found Keith five years earlier, and now it had found Ray. What did that time lag mean?

The trouble lived in his mind. He couldn't forget—how could he? How could anyone? But he was able to occasionally force what they'd done out of his mind by displacing it with other information, experiences, memories, music, TV, books, newspapers, and so on.

And Sugar … and a lot of alcohol.

But Ray's murder was the source of only half of the anxiety that was now rocketing through his nervous system—closing his throat, and draining the warmth from his hands and feet.

The other part was who had sent the text. The source of the text was worse—much worse—because he was alive and he was a threat. The other part was a name that had been gone from his life for years. Permanently, he had thought.

But he'd been wrong.

Chapter 5

We came up with a two-part strategy, and both parts required us all to do some setup work. My partners had to do what amounted to re-con—checking out our targets, and taking notes about their daily habits. Where did they go? What did they do? Who did they see? What days? What times? And we had to keep track of it all.

Google Drive has terrific tools for doing all of this—and the tools were always available to all of us, so we could update everything on the fly. Plan needs to change? No worries. We got it. Change the doc, and it changed for us all.

Thank you, Google!

Anyway, we had to do these things over long periods of time to make sure we had it all right—to make sure that all we noted were real parts of their lives.

Then came the hard part. We had to insert ourselves into their lives —specifically, into the places they went and the times they went there. This required a lot of trial and error—which was fine. We knew we were bound to get a lot wrong, and we were okay with that. This was a marathon, not a sprint. We could be in a place where and when we planned to kill one of them, and if it didn't work out? Fine. Maybe next time. There would always be a next time. We had plenty of time. We just wanted to get it right.

Time was on our side.

• • •

Dora had agreed to meet Fahira Long at 10 p.m. that night at the local P&W—the Pancake and Waffle House. The dogs had been walked and Missy was reading in bed. As she parked in the lot next to the restaurant, Dora spotted Long waiting outside, in a gray sweatshirt and matching sweatpants.

"How've you been?" Long asked, as they went inside.

"Hungry," Dora said.

"I could eat some waffles for sure," Long agreed.

"Pancakes for me," Dora replied. "Blueberry—with syrup."

"Yee-up."

The two women shuffled along the line, which stretched from the pick-up counter nearly to the door. A middle-aged woman with unruly sandy-colored hair was at the cashier waiting for a large take-out order while two hefty young women, one pale and freckled, the other dark-skinned with bright pink nails, put her order together and worked the registers. Both women were dressed in P&W uniforms—dark blue slacks, white polo shirts, and mauve aprons. They kept coming back to tell the customer that they were very sorry, but they were out of this or that item, so the order had to change several times.

This went on for about ten minutes, and then there was a wait as the adjusted order was prepared, to new specifications, placed into containers, and bagged.

Behind the customer was a line that included a crowd of young men who had, judging by their discussion, just come from seeing an action film at a nearby theatre. They were boisterous and filled with the kind of testosterone-driven energy that multiplies in intensity and volume with the number of young men in a group. They were also hungry and impatient.

After a few minutes, one of them yelled out, "Hey, how 'bout moving it along up there!" Followed by laughter from the group.

A minute later, one of his friends yelled, "Hey lady, c'mon! You're not going to eat all that!"

Another yelled, "Sure she is. Look at her!" Followed by more laughter and some of the boys turning toward the one who had spoken and suggesting he take a look at himself.

One of them, a dark-eyed tall boy with a medium build, a crimson T-shirt, blue jeans, and a light jacket, wasn't saying anything, but was glaring at the goings-on at the counter, his hands jammed into the side pockets of his jacket. He was watching the P&W employees, but his body and head were still. Only his eyes moved. His body was tensed.

The line of customers wound around a beige and brown free-standing combination garbage bin and countertop. On the counter sat two stacks of trays—used and unused—plastic cups and utensils, along with a potted plant as an end piece.

The young men were more and more restless. Their calls of "Come on!" and "We're waiting here!" had grown more virulent and demanding. The sandy-haired woman had been smiling sheepishly and holding up a hand urging patience, but now she was ignoring the young men entirely and tapping her feet, eager to take her food and leave the premises and the building storm behind her.

A plastic cup sailed over the waiting customers and landed on the counter.

The freckled employee turned her head quickly; her eyes scanned the line. She held up a finger. "We don't have to take that," she said. She looked out over the line; no one responded. She went back to work.

Another cup flew onto the counter, then another.

The dark-skinned employee had been closing the last of the containers and was about to place them all into several large bags for the customer. But she stopped working, was still for a moment, then whirled, grabbed a cup, and threw it back toward the group of young men.

"Whoa!" one of the group yelled, and a hail of cups flew toward the counter.

The young man in the dark T-shirt and jeans, his face clenched with rage, grabbed a food tray, curled it against his body like a Frisbee, and whipped it toward the counter, where it struck the freckled employee in the face. The woman turned away, covered her face with her hands, and shuffled toward the back of the kitchen, where two young men were working.

A thin man in a P&W uniform with bronze skin, medium-length black hair, and glasses stepped from the kitchen to the counter area, only to be hit in the face with another tray. He yelped and cringed away.

"What about our food!" yelled one of the young men in line.

The young man in the dark T-shirt who had thrown the first tray charged the counter.

Dora had seen enough. She quickly stepped in front of him, cutting him off, and he attempted to shove her away. Dora spun and pulled him toward her, then stepped aside, using his momentum to drive him into the counter, belly first. He pushed himself off and turned to face Dora, his face grim, mouth set.

"Don't do it," she warned, waving a finger. "Mistake," she added.

He grabbed at her finger, but she snapped her wrist back and flicked her fingers into his eyes. He cried out and turned back toward the counter, bending over it and moaning.

"Markey!" One of his friends yelled, and three of them rushed Dora, grabbing at her arms.

The first was met full in the face by Dora's front leg roundhouse kick and the laces and grommets of a No Bull trainer shoe, complete with tropical artwork on its side.

The second was met by the heel of the same shoe, which bounced off the face of the first, then snapped back against the nose of the second.

Long had stepped toward the fracas in a karate stance, but paused, then folded her arms, as she watched Dora handle the crew of young men.

As this was happening, the remaining counter woman slid the sandy-haired woman her packages, and the customer carefully picked her way between combatants and out the door.

"Shit!" the third of the friends muttered, as he and the rest of his friends gathered up their wounded and retreated out the side door of the restaurant.

The counterwoman who had served the customer disappeared into the food prep area and returned with the manager, as Dora and Long slapped hands. When they turned to face the counter, they found the manager smiling at them.

"Sorry to lose you a bunch of customers like that," Dora said.

The manager shrugged. "Happens in here sometimes. I like to think it's because our food's so irresistible. People can't wait to get their hands on it."

Long laughed. "Dora, this is Berto. Berto, meet Dora."

Dora extended a hand over the counter, but Berto pulled her into a hug, leaning toward her over the counter. She leaned toward him and returned the hug as best she could with the counter between them.

"Maybe we make up for it with a nice big nighttime breakfast," Long suggested, sending Dora a questioning look.

"Maybe so, Fahira," Berto said, "but neither of you are payin' so … what'll you have?"

• • •

Greg Walker went through the rest of his day like some kind of zombie, barely aware of what he was doing—the thinking part of his brain living in the past, reliving that terrible night.

He went about his errands and dealt with his day on autopilot. He politely greeted Johnny Ray, the Dorex delivery guy, but didn't return his ever-present smile. He just took the day's packages, turned, walked to his desk, and dropped them in a corner. It wasn't until he'd gone to the fridge for a beer that he felt the breeze and realized he'd left the front door open. That, and he smelled the exhaust from the Dorex delivery truck.

He'd gone to the dry cleaners and picked up two pairs of his trousers, the pink dress Sue had worn to dinner at the Club last Saturday, and Theo's white shirts. But when he came home, he left the clothes in his car. When Sue asked about the dry cleaning he had no idea what she was talking about. He was distracted and beside himself with fear.

There was an irony to his state of mind—an irony he thought he saw on Theo's face when Sue had asked about the dry cleaning. He was for-ever telling their son to "wake up and answer when he was spoken to" because Theo was forever playing his games—Grand Theft Auto (GTA) and PlayerUnknown's Battlegrounds (PUBG), and others. He and Sue agreed that Theo was too disconnected from reality to properly address the issues and responsibilities that came with being a high school se-nior—particularly his future. Did video games lead to real-world skills? Greg didn't think so, but if Theo never lived in the real world how would he ever find out?

But here he was, perhaps as disconnected as Theo was.

They were out of milk, so he drove to the ShopRite for more. As he drove, he remembered Ray once saying to him, "Greg, you quite clearly hate yourself, and self-loathing is not a good thing." The statement had angered Greg, who thought it arrogant, and he now recognized that it had been the beginning of the end of their friendship.

His response had been, "Well, I've been in therapy for 15 years learning to love myself. You're saying I've been wasting my money all this time—that my therapist is shit?"

Ray's answer to that had pissed him off even more. He'd said, "I'm telling you that you have a damn good reason for hating yourself."

He smiled wryly at the memory of his comeback: "Yeah, well, we all do, Ray."

And now Ray was dead. Murdered. Like Keith. Everyone who'd been a part of that night was being eliminated and he was pretty sure who was responsible and why.

He parked in the supermarket lot and went into the store, trying to remember if they were running low on anything else, then realized that anything he might buy other than milk was likely to be the wrong brand, flavor, or size as far as Sue was concerned. Her shopping list was extremely specific.

On the drive back, his mind drifted to the good times—the parties, the meetings, the golf, the bowling. He thought of guys he never saw anymore—of Sylvester teaching little Seth to bowl; the ball had been as big as the little boy, who had pushed the ball and run alongside it, until it knocked down a single pin, and then stopped. Little Seth had very nearly been scooped up by the pinsetter, as it cleared the rest of the pins. Oh, how that boy had cried.

Greg laughed to himself as he pulled into his driveway, then remembered the text and stopped laughing.

• • •

Missy found two Earl Lincolns in her reverse lookup database, and Dora called them both. The first was a twenty-two-year-old kid who sold auto accessories—primarily surround-sound audio for used cars. Once Dora determined he was not the Earl Lincoln she was looking for, he tried to sell her a system for her turbo and wouldn't let her get a word in to explain that she had no interest in sound systems. He wouldn't shut up, so she hung up on him.

She tried the second number Missy gave her.

"Is this Earl Lincoln?"

"Who wants to know?" The man's voice was low and gravelly, as though he was or had been a smoker.

"My name is Dora Ellison. I work for Geller Investigations in Beach City."

"Okay."

"Is this Earl Lincoln?"

"What's this in reference to?"

"Ray Drucker."

"Oh, boy." She could practically hear him drag his palm down his face, over his mouth and chin.

"So this is Earl Lincoln?"

 A Divisive Storm

"Yeah, it is."

"I'm sorry to have to tell you, but Mr. Drucker is dead." She wanted to hear his reaction.

"Aw, hell. How did he die?"

She redirected the conversation. "You had a … challenged relationship with Mr. Drucker, isn't that so?"

"Well, I was his immediate supervisor. So it sort of came with the territory."

"He was not a great employee?"

"You could say that."

"I understand he was let go because he drank on the job."

"That's correct."

"Which affected his pension, which he wasn't happy about."

"Well, he smelled of alcohol on the job—more than once. I couldn't very well keep him on."

"How did he react when you let him go?"

Lincoln grunted. "He came at me—verbally, I mean. Said I had it in for him—that losing his job would ruin his pension—which it didn't. He did get at least some of it. Anyway, the truth was I let him skate more than once."

"His wife says he was sensitive and had depression."

"Well, he was sensitive—prickly's more like it. Apt to fly off the handle. Of course, that might have been the alcohol talking. Hell, maybe the booze calmed him down. But that wasn't my problem. I have a department to run. Far as his medical records—depression and like that—I couldn't say. Probably a HIPAA issue."

"Any idea who might have wanted to kill him?"

"Kill him? He was murdered? Christ!"

"He was."

"No, I don't. Tell you the truth, I didn't like him very much, but I wasn't there to make friends. I was his supervisor and I had to run a tight ship. The county demands it, and he ran afoul of the process by virtue of his drinking. Can't have that at county. Years ago it was different, but it isn't years ago anymore, is it?"

"I guess not. Well, thank you, Mr. Lincoln."

Chapter 6

The second part of the plan was something I had to do myself, and it required physical contact with the targets—which was really, really hard because I wanted to shove a knife into them every time I saw them. Really. Every time I saw any of them, my mind just shut off and I got filled up with this "gotta kill him right fucking now" urge that was so strong. So powerful. So hard to resist—and yet I did. I had waited five years between the first two. Five fucking years—and I could wait five more if it came to it. I could do that because I killed them in my mind every day. Every. Fucking. Day.

Besides, I had to resist if I wanted to kill them. I couldn't just do it when I felt like it, no matter how much I wanted to. We had a plan, and we needed to stick to it.

The second part of this plan—the one that was all on me—was not about killing them; it was about holding them accountable for what they did. It was about proving that they'd done what they'd done. It was about evidence.

I had two kinds of evidence in mind. One was real, existing evidence of what they'd done. I was pretty sure I had some—at least I thought I had some chance of having some, and I set about keeping it safe for the day when I could use it. This wasn't my idea, it was the idea of one of the very few people I trusted. Not one of my partners in crime—someone else. Someone whose trust was without question.

Then there was the second kind of evidence. This evidence wasn't real, but so what? To catch and put away these pieces of shit, I had to become a piece of shit myself. If they were killed—which was plan number one—it would be worth it, and if they were put away for doing what they'd done to me—plan number two—that would be worth it too, despite not being the priority.

The ends justified the fucking means. It sure as hell did!

And this one took some doing. I had to put myself in a position to set up evidence to put these fucks away for what they did. I had to think hard to come up with this part of the plan, and my partners helped. We put our heads together and we came up with a great plan. Plan number two. We figured out how I could put myself in a position to gather evidence, and to plant that evidence.

There's nothing like a good fucking plan, especially when it leads to justice … and revenge.

• • •

Dennis McCrae was a fit 60-year-old with blond hair that was going gray and bright blue eyes that crinkled at the corners. He was working under the hood of a red vintage Corvette and joking with another mechanic who was hidden, except for his legs, beneath a much newer blue one. Both were laughing as Dora came in, introduced herself, and explained why she was there.

"Let me tell you about Ray Drucker," McCrae said. They had moved to his office, which smelled of grease and chewing gum. "You couldn't talk to the guy. He would get an idea into his head and no matter how wrong it was, he'd run with it until he ran right off the edge of a cliff."

Laughter came through the door from beneath the blue Stingray. "You're telling me!"

"My understanding is that the two of you argued—about business."

McCrae, who had been smiling, turned serious. He nodded. "Look," he held out a palm, "I made a mistake. I wrote up a bill of sale and I forgot about a part—I think it was a set of shocks that were really high-end. I'm human. We'd known each other for decades. We were friends, or I thought we were. But boy, when I told him about this, he wouldn't hear it, went off like I was trying to rip him off, rip his family off." McCrae shook his head. "I'd've taken half. But you couldn't tell Ray anything."

"Any idea who might want to hurt him?"

"Any idea who wouldn't?" came the cheerful voice from under the blue car.

"Easy, Smitty," McCrae called, then looked at Dora, who was watching his expression carefully. "Honestly, no. And Smitty's kidding. I read about what happened. There was an article the next morning, then a bigger one today." He pressed his lips together. "It's a shame. We were friends. I thought he turned into a bit of a prick at the end, but he was hard up for money, you know? And that can change a person."

It was late afternoon and Dora drove home with her window half open so she could breathe in the sweet smell of blossoming flowers and with it, the excitement of early spring. Missy was already waiting on the sidewalk.

"I fed the dogs and took them out," Missy said, as she opened the passenger door and got in. "They say hi."

They set off in Dora's Subaru turbo for the beachfront apartment shared by their friends Charlie Bernelli and his wife, Christine Pearsall, who was also the mayor of Beach City, one of only a handful of cities on Long Island. The two held dinners every couple of weeks for a group of friends that included Dora and Missy. Charlie's son, Charlie Bernelli III —nicknamed C3—was often present, along with his longtime girlfriend, Sarah Turner, the editor of the *Beach City Chronicle*.

"I have a question," Dora said. "Let's say a guy with a business was having money problems. How could that affect his behavior?"

Missy shrugged. "That's not a lot of information to go by, but … all sorts of ways. Is he married? Does he have kids? We're talking about Ray Drucker, right?"

"Yeah, and he is, and he does—or did. As you know, he owned a gun shop and shooting range—used to work for the county as a clerk."

"Well," Missy began, "the obvious, I guess. He might max out his credit cards, go into debt, fall behind on his taxes—that sort of thing. If he's used to hanging around with certain people, he might go to a loan shark or get involved in some criminal activity." Missy looked at Dora. "Make sense?"

Dora nodded and grunted, but didn't answer.

Missy asked, "Why do you think he had money problems? Did his wife say so? Did his wife share his credit card bills with you?"

Dora shook her head. "The Corvette guy he had that fight with, the one Katie told us about, had that impression. That their disagreement was the tip of the iceberg."

After finding a parking spot a half block from Charlie and Christine's beachfront building, Dora and Missy stepped into the chrome and marble lobby and were buzzed up to the penthouse.

• • •

C3 opened the apartment door and held out his arms. Dora hugged the fit young man with the shaggy blond hair and they swayed in a tight embrace. C3 hugged Missy in a lighter, more perfunctory way and gave her a quick kiss on the cheek. Then he stepped back and held the door as they entered the enormous apartment.

"Ooh, something smells good!" Missy exclaimed.

"Mussels marinara," C3 explained.

Missy shook her head, squinting and concentrating. "But there's also … something with breading and garlic."

"Breaded stuffed artichokes!" Christine called from the couch. The auburn-haired, forty-something mayor had reclined to a near-lying down position amidst a half dozen pillows, her pregnancy apparent, and her belly rising among the pillows like a small, round mountain. Her red blouse did not quite cover her, and a pale pink crescent of flesh was visible between two of the pillows.

Dora and Missy stepped into the luxury townhouse's expansive living room and dinette, with its floor-to-ceiling windows that overlooked the boardwalk and beach, and its sunken double-crescent couches and winding staircase to the second floor.

With Christine were her husband, Charlie Bernelli Jr., his son C3, and C3's girlfriend, Sarah Turner. All were arrayed on the twin couches; the cushioned circular table between them held a tray festooned with drinks and finger foods.

Charlie rose and held out his arms in much the same way his son had. He shared his son's lionesque, swept-back hairstyle, though his was more gray than blond. In one hand, he grasped a glass of scotch on the rocks. Dora and Missy hugged him while C3 fetched a couple of chairs from the dining room table. Christine waved.

"Hey, Dor. Missy," Sarah called; she was dressed in her usual black ensemble, her long dark hair tied back in a ponytail.

"Drinks?" C3 asked as he arrived with the chairs.

"Beer," Dora said. "Bottled preferably."

"We have—" he began.

"Surprise me," Dora interrupted, as C3 looked at Missy, eyebrows raised.

"White wine," Missy said.

"How are you feeling?" Dora asked Christine.

Christine smiled ruefully. "Complicated question. I feel more or less okay. The morning sickness is long gone. I'm all over the place emotionally. I'm excited, I'm scared, I'm nauseous, I'm terrified."

"When are you due?" Missy asked as C3 returned with her wine. He sat down next to Sarah and they clasped hands.

Christine looked at her watch. "Any minute!" She laughed at Missy's look of alarm. "Actually, Thursday." She nodded toward one of several kitchen countertops on the far side of the dinette. "Besides what you see here, there are more crudités, cheese and crackers, shrimp, anchovies, roasted peppers, and eggplant. So help yourselves."

"Don't mind if I do," Dora rose and headed in that direction. Missy followed. They returned several minutes later with plates of food.

"So, I have a question for you guys," Dora said. "If you were in business and money was tight, how would that affect your behavior?"

"Am I a criminal?" Charlie wanted to know.

"Well," his wife said, "you're not the most ethical person I know."

Charlie laughed easily, as did Sarah.

Dora thought about the question. "Let's say you're open to a variety of options."

"If you're running a business," Charlie said, sipping his scotch thoughtfully, "you might raise prices or try to grow the business by adding salespeople, product—that sort of thing."

"What if those were not options?" Missy asked.

"You could cheat," Charlie added.

"Is this related to a case?" C3 wanted to know. He was in his third year of sobriety and was drinking ginger ale, as was Sarah, who was not in recovery but was supporting his sobriety.

"Can't say," Dora answered.

"Are you involved in the Ray Drucker murder case?" Charlie asked.

Dora was careful to keep her facial expression neutral. "Couldn't tell you if I was." She shrugged.

"That's a yes!" Charlie proclaimed.

"Charles…" Christine gave him a withering look that told him to back off.

Charlie turned to Sarah, who was leaning against C3. Their hands remained clasped on her knee. "I read what you wrote about the murder in the *Chronicle*. Wouldn't you think someone would have seen a person who just walks up to a car, pulls out a pistol, and shoots the driver? This was in a pretty well-lit parking lot." Sarah had been the editor and part-owner of *The Beach City Chronicle,* the local online newspaper, for nearly three years, since the previous owner had been caught up in a murder cover-up.

Sarah's eyes narrowed as she considered the question. "Well, it was nighttime and the person wore a hoodie and dark clothing. The police have seen the drugstore's video. I'm not aware of anyone having seen the person in the store, walking away, or driving away, if that's what you mean."

Charlie swirled his drink, then drained the remaining scotch. "This is a busy town at night and that's a busy area with a luncheonette next door and doctors' offices across the street. Someone ought to have seen something."

Christine gave a loud sigh. "Could we stop talking about this, Charles? It's giving me agita." As the mayor of Beach City, Christine was vocal about her opinion that extensive news coverage of violent crimes hurt the tourist industry, which was one of Beach City's primary sources of revenue and commerce.

Charlie made a "who me?" face, then turned and walked to the bar to refill his drink.

Sarah was looking thoughtfully at Christine. Both women held their current positions as the result of a murder three years earlier that had deposed their predecessors. Despite being *de facto* in-laws, the two often clashed, though amicably, over the *Chronicle*'s coverage of violent crime, which Christine complained was too graphic. Sarah believed that her job was to keep the public informed and to include details of crimes that might help solve them. The two agreed that news stories about neighborhood crimes might impact local tourism, the city's most important industry, but they differed on how best to address that issue.

"I'm doing my best to walk that line," Sarah explained. "I get that you'd just want stats in the news. But on March 17—"

"Saint Paddy's Day," C3 added.

"—at 9:30 p.m., in the parking lot of Evergreen Drugs, one Ray Drucker was murdered via gunshot wound to the eye—"

"To the eye?" Missy groaned. "Didn't know that."

Sarah nodded. "How do I not print that?"

Christine's eyes widened. "That's exactly the story we don't want." She nodded toward Missy. "What if Missy was someone who was planning to come to Beach City for dinner with her—" she hesitated, glancing at Dora, "—with her girlfriend, and say, to a concert on the boardwalk. And maybe they would buy some ice cream and get cozy—maybe even stay at the Beach City Hotel."

Dora and Missy glanced at one another. Dora waggled her eyebrows.

Christine continued. "But then they see this gory reportage of murder that mentions a shot in the eye being the cause of death, and they get grossed out and go elsewhere. Your reporting loses us significant business."

Charlie, who had returned with his drink, stood behind Christine, his hand squeezing her shoulder, trying to keep her calm.

Sarah pressed her lips together and looked into her lap, where C3 was stroking her hand with his thumb. "Christine, I get your position, but you've got to get mine. I've got to write about what's going on. I have a responsibility to keep the public informed. I also have a responsibility, perhaps unsaid, to the police, to put enough information out there for someone who might have been in the vicinity and might have seen something, to come forward and say so. That kind of thing could lead to putting a murderer behind bars." A passionate journalist, Sarah was leaning forward now, her eyes focused, her jaw set and thrust slightly forward.

Christine sighed. "You also have a responsibility to your advertisers to draw eyes to the pages or whatever you call your online content, to help sell ads." She was exasperated and trying hard not to show it. "Anyway … maybe you can tone it down a little."

Sarah perked up, cocked her head, and looked at Christine, her eyes sparkling. "Wait, wait. I have an idea. While I have to cover the news, I also happen to agree with you. We *are* a community newspaper in a community where tourism is important and crime can be disruptive. How about if I did two specific things going forward—a series on our wonderful tourist attractions, and another that uncovers sources of crime?"

"Well," Christine grumbled. "Not too sure about the second…"

"It would be a service—I'd talk to the police, look at where the crime is coming from, and what can be done about it." She leaned further forward, her elbows on her knees. "Look, crime comes from all over. But more of it comes from late-night drinkers who are driving drunk or wandering around, or from the restaurants, the high school— kids being kids and getting out of hand. Some of it comes from poorer areas of town, where a few bad apples ruin it for the majority, who are good people. How can this be bad?"

"Hah!" Christine exclaimed. "Wait and see! Someone's going to call racism!" She obviously had more to say as she struggled to sit up, thrashing amidst the pillows, and pulling her legs in then thrusting them out in an effort to right herself. Charlie had put his drink down and was gently pulling her back from behind, his hands on either side of her neck. He kissed her hair, which was reddish, curly, and just short of shoulder length. Her face too had reddened; she had one palm on her belly, which she began rubbing in smooth circles.

Dora gave Sarah a polite, gentle look. "How is Livvie doing?" She was trying to calm the conversation. Livvie was C3 and Sarah's two-year-old daughter, who had been born with Down syndrome but was otherwise healthy.

Sarah smiled at Dora, grateful for the change in subject. "She's at Vanessa's, playing with Drew and Buster. Kelvin's there too—if I know him, he's probably got them all singing."

"She's obsessed with the idea of getting a dog," C3 said, smiling. "It's all she talks about."

"You're getting a dog?" Dora was delighted. When she and Missy moved in together they blended their households, which consisted of their dogs, Comfort and Freedom; the latter Dora had liberated from her violent owner. The mismatched canines were now inseparable, with Comfort the tiny drill sergeant and Freedom the obedient, somewhat clumsy giant.

"No!" C3 and Sarah answered together.

"We're not getting a dog," Sarah said emphatically. "But Liv doesn't want to hear it," she added.

"And at this point," C3 added, "neither do we."

"Why not bring her over to us and she can visit with ours," Dora suggested.

Missy added, "She can pretend they're hers for an hour or two."

Sarah's eyes sparkled, and she pointed at Dora and Missy. "We'll take you up on that!"

"Oh, boy!" Christine moaned and rolled to one side. She'd begun panting. "Ohhh!" She curled into a fetal position and grasped her belly with her right hand curving along the bottom and her left hand rubbing circles on top.

From behind the couch, Charlie bent over her, his face next to hers. "Is it time? Is it now?" He rushed around and knelt next to her, his palm on the back of her neck, pulling her head to his shoulder.

She was still for a long moment. Everyone looked at Christine. The room had hushed, except for Christine's loud panting.

"Breathe slowly," Charlie said, his voice shaking. "Deep cleansing breaths."

"Ooohhh," Christine gasped; moans came from deep within her, bursting from her lips as though propelled by some powerful, painful pump. "Charrrliiie! Charrrliiie!"

"I'm here, baby. Right here!" He bent so close to her face that his hair tumbled onto her cheeks.

"Get off me!" she growled.

"What can I do?" Charlie looked around frantically.

"Charrrliiie!"

"Yeah, baby? Take a cleansing breath!"

"Fuck that!" She grasped his collar with her free fist and yanked him close. "Get me to the fuckin' hospital!"

Chapter 7

One important part of our plan was that I had to be the one who would do the actual killing. Otherwise, what was the point? Justice. Revenge. And if one of them did it, neither of those would be there for me. I was the one who wanted justice, so I was the one who would have to pull the trigger.

I had to learn to use a gun. No problem. Easy enough. I didn't have to learn to be all that accurate. I was going to put the gun right up to the sides of their faces. I needed them to see who was killing them, and why. I needed to see them recognize me—and to see their fear. That was part and parcel of the whole deal.

So no accuracy was necessary. I was going to walk right up to them, probably when they were in their cars, doing some everyday thing in a public place—but, and this was really important, I'd show up when no one was close to them. I had to be able to get back in my car—which would have different stolen plates for each killing—same car, different plates—and just drive the fuck away.

I was going to wear something that covered my face—a hoodie, probably. We'd talked about this. And I was going to keep the gun in my pocket until I was right there next to them, and they saw who I was. Then I'd make sure they saw the gun because I needed them to know that they were about to die.

Then I'd put the gun right up to their faces, and I'd pull the trigger.

Then, I'd simply walk away.

And on to the next one.

• • •

On Saturday evening, Dora and Missy drove into New York City to see a Broadway show. The traffic on the Long Island Expressway was, as usual, terrible. In the car on the way in, Missy asked, "How've you been feeling?"

Dora looked back at her, confused. "What do you mean?"

"The anxiety? The PTSD? The dreams?"

Dora didn't answer; she just raised her eyebrows and continued driving for a few minutes. "Oh. Well."

Missy watched her, waiting.

"Somewhat better."

Missy raised an encouraging eyebrow. "Yeah?"

"I think going to Shay's and that … altercation at the P&W were good for me. What's not good for me is lying around."

"Okay," Missy said. "I guess."

"And you?"

"Me?"

"How're you doing?"

Missy laughed. "You wake up next to me every morning. You know how I'm doing."

Dora gave her a sideways, dubious look. "Yeah? How's your father doing?"

"Oh."

"Yeah, oh."

Missy looked out the window as they inched past a tractor-trailer. They were driving through a section of Queens in which many of the stores and offices had Chinese signs. "He's still tearing paper into little bits, only now my mother gets to the mail before he does. He's doing it with napkins. The cat apparently loves it. My mother's really stressed. He doesn't wash or bathe or shave, and he refuses to get a haircut. Bai's husband, Mingzé, spends all his time running the company and making sure my father doesn't do anything crazy—like speak to clients."

"How does Mingzé manage that?"

Missy shook her head with a look of despair. "I have no idea. He doesn't have the connection to the clients my father does. My father's the one who brought in the clients in the first place. He knows them, and they trust him. But he's not someone you can trust right now. He's kind of like a five-year-old." She folded her arms across her chest. "The whole thing's a mess."

Dora glanced at Missy. "Consider yourself lucky you have a family."

Missy looked back at her and responded dryly. "You've got to be kidding."

• • •

The play itself had been the subject of recent controversy, which was part of their reason for attending. After the show, Dora and Missy returned to the turbo and exchanged a look.

"Well, that was weird." Missy rolled her tongue around the inside of her mouth and raised her eyebrows while Dora drove out of the lot and onto 46th Street heading east across Manhattan.

"The show was great!" Dora responded.

"I mean what happened before the show. Scary!"

Dora looked at Missy and laid a hand on her thigh. "No one's going to hurt you, babe."

Missy gave a reassured smile. "I know, but still—what did they hope to gain by trying to tell theatregoers 'the real story behind the Jew the play is about?' What was the point? What were they hoping to gain?"

"Notoriety. What's the point of any hate group? To harass and scare you. To get their name out there. That's literally the definition of terrorism—they're out to terrorize."

"Well, they succeeded with me." Missy shook her head.

They were quiet for a few blocks. Eventually, they turned onto Second Avenue, heading downtown. "So, what you asked before," Dora said, "I'm still having those nightmares." She swallowed. "She's attacking me, and I can't move. I wake up and can't get back to sleep. Then the whole next day, I'm looking over my shoulder, and I get this kind of creepy feeling I can't shake."

"Know what'll help?" Missy said, "Listen to comedy. Go to YouTube or Spotify and find a comedy special. Something else you can do.

Meditate. Focus on your breath. Just notice it, and when your attention wanders to something else, bring it back. Then focus on the ground or the bed or couch holding you up. Those things, and your breath—are literally supporting you. Think about that. They've got you. I've got you."

Dora smiled. "I appreciate that. I'll do it." She repeated to herself. "Meditate and listen to comedy." She looked at Missy. "I also have another idea—a more physical idea."

Missy looked at her with a sideways glance.

"No, not that—but that, too." Dora laughed. "This is something else."

After they'd driven another few minutes, Missy asked, "Why do you want to do this?"

Dora glanced at her. "Do what?"

"Continue investigating. You've put some bad people away. Why not stop?"

Dora continued to drive. Finally, she sucked air in between her teeth. "I guess I need to see things turn out okay for other people." She sighed. "I've gotta try to make their things turn out better than my things."

"Because your things didn't?"

"Something like that."

Missy took her hand. "We're still working on your things, babe."

• • •

"So, this is where Ray Drucker hung out," Missy said, her voice echoing in the John Farmer Club's cavernous foyer.

"Quite the old money look," Dora observed.

"Hmm," Missy said, eyeing the Greek statuettes, all of which were of naked men. "Wonder why there are no women?"

"I'm sure there's a reason," Dora said, sounding quite certain.

They walked through the bar, then through a set of heavy oak double doors which were propped open. Inside was a freestanding maître d' counter where a tall, willowy blonde woman stood. "Two?" She asked, smiling, then squinted at Missy a little too long.

Missy leaned toward Dora. "Something wrong with my clothes?"

Dora shook her head. "Nope." Dora shook her head again, this time at the maître d'. "We're meeting a gentleman—Adam Geller?"

"Ah." The woman nodded. "They're here."

"*They're…?*" Dora whispered.

The maître d' led Dora and Missy to a table where Adam and Thelma, his office manager, were waiting.

"Thelma!" Missy bent to kiss the conservatively dressed woman, but Thelma arched away.

"Please!" Her small dark eyes glanced at the newcomers from within her pained face.

"We didn't know you'd be here," Dora said affably.

"Didn't know dinosaurs like me ate, you mean," Thelma continued, her tone the same flat, loud, braying honk she used at work. Diners throughout the restaurant turned, startled.

"It's nice to see you ladies out of the office for a change," Adam said, and Dora noticed that he seemed to have regained a bit of his pallor. Adam was sixty-six and had suffered a challenging few years, health-wise. He'd replaced both hips, had spinal fusion surgery to stave off paralysis, and had an emergency abdominal resection which left him with a temporary colostomy bag—now reversed. Ten months earlier he'd been diagnosed with prostate cancer, which had been treated with radiation. His health had been one of the main reasons he had taken on Dora and Missy as part-time, now nearly full-time investigators—though Missy retained a "now and then" research librarian position at the Beach City Library.

"Weren't Christine and Charlie coming with their kids?" Adam asked.

"I told you, old man," Thelma scolded. "They're at the hospital with Christine. Charlie's with her and his son and Sarah Turner went along as moral support." Thelma made it her business to know all local gossip and nearly everything else worth knowing in the Beach City environs.

"We called our friend Vanessa and asked her to come," Missy began.

"And…?" Thelma asked.

"She said, 'The John Farmer Club? I can't go there.'"

"I asked her why not," Dora continued. "And Vanessa told me, "'You really don't know?' I said, 'I don't.' She said, 'Ask around.'"

"I'll tell you why," Adam said. "It's kind of an old boys' club."

"I can see that." Dora glanced around the restaurant, which was done in polished wood paneling with ornate wall sconces mounted every twelve feet about six feet off the ground. The sconces threw off a yellow light that lent a golden caste to the polished wood walls, an effect that was heightened by the gold and white paneling on the high ceilings.

Dora shrugged. "But so what?"

"An old, white, boys' club," Adam added.

Dora raised her eyebrows and nodded slowly. "Ohhh."

Missy's eyes darted anxiously around the room. "Well, I'm not old, I'm not a boy, and I'm not white." She smirked nervously. "And yet, here I am."

"You'll be fine," Dora assured her.

"So, if Vanessa didn't want to come here," Adam said to Dora, "why didn't you give us a call? We could have met you someplace else."

Dora shook her head. "I wanted to find out what she meant." She leaned across the table, toward Adam and Thelma. "And I've gotta say, everyone here does look pretty white."

"There was another reason," Missy said. "The victim in our case, Ray Drucker, apparently used to come here with some old friends."

"Do you mean he used to come here back when he had those friends," Adam asked, "or do you mean he came here recently with old friends, as in renewing those friendships?"

"Or, did he come here with friends who are old," Thelma added, grinning at Adam.

"Touché," said Adam.

Dora blinked. "I'm not sure. We'll have to ask his wife."

"If racial exclusivity is the theme of the night," Missy said, "listen to what happened at the play we just saw."

Thelma was looking at Missy. "What the hell is racial exclusivity?" she asked, her tone no-nonsense. "You mean racism."

Missy thinned her lips and held out her hands, her fingers splayed. "I was being polite," she murmured.

"Nothing polite about racism," Thelma responded, shaking her head.

"You don't have to tell me," Missy said.

"We went to see a Broadway play," Dora said, "called *Parade*. It's based on a true story about a Jewish guy in Marietta, Georgia named Leo Frank who was wrongly jailed and lynched for supposedly raping a 13-year-old girl who worked for him. Except, he didn't do it."

"I've heard of it," Adam said, nodding sadly. "It's a revival. It was originally staged in the 90s."

"That's right," Missy said.

"While we were in line," Dora said, "a bunch of creeps in ski masks came over and tried to hand out leaflets that trashed Leo Frank."

"Antisemitism," Adam noted, with a sad smile. "Some things never change."

"It was scary!" Missy exclaimed. Dora took her hand.

"But you went in? You saw the show?" Adam asked.

Dora and Missy nodded.

"Good," said Thelma.

Adam said, "It's now more than a hundred years after that story took place, and yet there was bigotry at the performance!" Adam's head twitched several times to the right.

"Are you okay?" Dora asked.

Thelma subtly shook her head at her.

Adam muttered something out of the right side of his mouth. "It sure is," was what he said, but he said it so softly he could hardly be heard.

Suddenly, Adam slid his chair back and stood up. "Excuse me." He stood, looked around, and walked toward a sign indicating the restrooms.

"What was that about?" Dora asked.

Thelma sighed. "He talks to his wife, who's been gone a few years. He's been doing it for a while, but it's gotten worse since his cancer. He thinks he's joining her soon."

"But I thought his radiation was successful," Dora protested.

Thelma nodded. "It was." She held her hands out to either side, a "what can you do" gesture. "All you can do is ignore it." She brightened. "Even better, you can go over the case."

"But we're out to dinner!" Dora complained.

Thelma shrugged. "The only thing that approaches his love for his late wife is his obsession with work."

Adam returned and with a stealthy glance to his right, sat down again.

"We were hoping you could shed some light on this new case," Dora offered and Missy nodded in agreement.

"I can try," Adam offered.

"Here's what we know so far. Ray Drucker got a text from Evergreen Drugs on Park and Evergreen, that some medication was ready. So he went there at eight-thirty on St. Patrick's night, to pick it up. He parked in the lot, where the store's video camera records a Prius parking next to his Equinox. A person in a dark hoodie gets out and walks over to his car. Recognizing that person, Drucker rolls down his window, and the person shoots him in the face, killing him. Then that person gets back into their car and drives away. Drucker's family relationships are apparently normal. He's a husband, a father, and a grandfather."

Adam grunted and looked sharply to his right. "I was going to ask," he complained. "What was he doing just prior to going to the drugstore?"

"He was watching a murder mystery on Netflix with his wife, Katie," Dora answered.

A waiter appeared, handed out menus, and took drink orders.

Adam's eyes were focused on Dora; they flicked to his right, then back to Dora. "Work situation?"

"Worked as a filing clerk for the county until his boss realized he'd been drinking on his lunch break and he was let go."

"Did he lose his pension?"

Dora equivocated. "It was reduced, but not lost, which pissed him off. We've already met with his former supervisor, who was shocked that he was murdered."

"Had he ever been known to drink on his lunch break before?"

"Yes," Dora said. "And in the morning."

"Was he out of work long?"

"We're not exactly sure, but he purchased a gun shop and shooting range at auction that had been previously owned by one Thomas Bannion."

"You may remember," Missy said, "Thomas Bannion was involved in supplying guns around the island—illegally, I mean."

"How's that business doing now?"

"Seems to be doing well, far as we can tell," said Dora.

Adam's eyes had grown more and more active, bouncing from each of them to spots around the room. "What about the victim's social life?"

"The victim and his wife spent much of their time with one another."

Adam grunted.

"Oh, there's this," Missy said, suddenly. "The victim was involved in the purchase of a car from one…" She closed her eyes, thinking, "Dennis McCrae."

"Oh, the 'Vette Guy," Adam said.

"Right!" Dora agreed.

"He'd bought a Corvette from the guy," Missy explained, "and the guy tried to come back and change the price because he said he'd forgotten it had some fancy shock absorbers."

"They had a pretty big argument, apparently," Dora said. "But to get gunned down in a parking lot over it—especially after the argument was over. In other words, not in the heat of the moment." She shook her head. "Premeditation based on that? Possible, but I don't think so."

"I wouldn't be so sure," said Adam. "What was the difference in price?"

"Mid-four digits," Missy answered.

Adam nodded. "What else?"

"The victim didn't have many friends outside the marriage."

"Did they have friends as a couple?"

Dora shook her head.

Adam squinted, dubious. "The victim had no friends?"

"The victim used to come here. His friends were here."

Adam's eyebrows went up. "Here…" He seemed to see the room for the first time. He took a long moment, slowly looking around. "This place is right out of the 1950s, or before."

"Got that right," Thelma agreed.

Adam thought of something. "Who would have known Ray Drucker was going to the drugstore at eight-thirty that night?"

Dora and Missy looked at one another. "His wife?" Dora said.

"Maybe someone at Evergreen," Missy added.

"Any idea of who he hung around with when he used to come here?" Adam's eyes were piercing now; he was on a roll or thought he was.

"According to his wife, three guys. Wayne, Keith, and Greg."

"Last names?"

"Not yet," Dora said.

"Work on them," Adam said. "And find out about any conflicts at the gun range. And did anyone at Evergreen know about the prescription, or is that automated?"

"What we're wondering," Dora said, "is why someone would want to kill this guy?"

Adam gave a crooked smile. "Dora, you know what I'm going to ask you, right?"

She smiled back, nodding. "What are the most common reasons for murdering people?"

"Love and money," they said together.

Adam continued. "The guy's middle-aged, married—happily it would seem, though you can't assume that's true. Probably not love—though could be lust. Could be he has something on the side, but that doesn't smell right here. So, what about his business? There's some stuff you need to look at there, for sure. But then, look at these old friends. That's my take."

He smiled—a real smile, as the waiter took their orders. It was the happiest he had looked all evening. Dora saw that Adam was looking at the waiter, curiosity on his face. He then glanced furtively to his right and said a quick word out of the corner of his mouth.

"Look around," he said. "What do you see?" Not sure whom he was speaking to, Dora and Missy, and even Thelma scanned the room. He added, "But really look."

"I see a very upscale restaurant where well-off people are eating dinner," Dora answered.

"What else?"

"Waiters and waitresses," Missy added.

"And?"

"Busboys," Thelma added. "Nice looking busboys. I wouldn't kick any of them out of bed."

Adam gave his office manager a derisive look. "You probably wouldn't kick anyone out of bed."

She turned on him, one eyebrow raised, the other cocked low over an eye. "Don't flatter yourself, old man."

Adam laughed heartily, then said, "What shared characteristics do many of the staff share?"

Missy shrugged. "Well, they seem to be white."

"The busboys are all buff," Thelma insisted, with a glare at her boss.

Dora looked around. The waitresses were a mix of blonde and brunette; one had auburn hair with reddish highlights. The waiters and busboys were all-American football types. Some had Nordic features. A few might have been Greek or Italian-American. None that she could see were Black or Latin American, and Thelma was right—the busboys and several waiters were husky, with enormous shoulders, and bulging arm and leg muscles. The rest looked athletic as well.

The question was, what did any of this mean, and what, if anything, did any of it have to do with Ray Drucker's murder?

Chapter 8

Killing them was absolutely fantastic. It was freedom. I was broken. Ruined. Now I was on top of the fucking world. Unless you've been through something as horrible as what I've been through, you just don't know. Guilt. Shame. Terror. Will they come back? Was it my fault?

Months of that shit. Years of that shit. I couldn't even begin to think about doing anything about it for a long, long time. I was just putting one foot in front of the other. I was just surviving. Even when I shared my secret with others, I wasn't yet doing anything about it. Even when we had a plan and started executing it, we still weren't really doing anything about it—even though we were. There was no justice. Yet.

So, after finally taking care of the first one—the joy was incredible—Christmas. The Fourth of July. My birthday. It was such a damn relief. We finally got one.

But then we had to wait before going after another. We had to be sure we covered our tracks. And we did.

And it was the same with the second one. And every bit as sweet and worth the wait.

Time for number three.

* * *

Charlie had driven Christine to the emergency ward at the Beach City Medical Center. C3 and Sarah drove separately, stopping at home to pay the sitter and pick up Livvie, since they had no idea how long they'd be at the hospital. When they arrived, they were surprised to find Charlie in the waiting room.

When he saw his father through the double doors, C3 hurried into the lobby, leaving Sarah walking slowly into the building with Livvie, who stopped every now and then to point at whatever drew her attention.

"What're you doing out in the lobby?" C3 asked.

Charlie's lips were pressed together, his lower lip covering the upper and his face in a frightened grimace. "Something's wrong. She started having convulsions and they're making me wait out here." His eyes were bulging and he was glancing around in a panic.

"What do you mean, convulsions?"

Charlie whipped his head from one side to the other, reached into the front of his pants, and pulled out a pint of whiskey. He took several swallows and stuffed it back into his pants, as his head shook like a dog coming in out of the rain.

"How should I know?" he shouted. "They haven't told me shit!"

Sarah and Livvie had caught up to them. Sarah rested her palm gently on Charlie's upper arm. "She's in the best possible place then, Charlie—a hospital. Did the triage nurse say anything about what might be causing her symptoms?"

Charlie calmed slightly, pulled the bottle out and took another swallow, then bubbled his lips. "Ahh—she has high blood pressure. The nurse thought that could be related. She said a bunch of bullshit—I don't know!"

Sarah's voice was preternaturally calm, as though she were talking to a spooked horse or a panicked child. "Why do you say it's bullshit?"

He looked at her, and for a moment, C3 thought he was going to hit her. But instead, he said, "Medical gibberish!" He barked a laugh. "I know bullshit when I hear it. Hey, I'm in advertising. I live on bullshit!" He grew suddenly serious. "I think they said something about 'clamps in her.'"

There was silence for several seconds, then Sarah asked with concern, "Eclampsia?"

Charlie pointed a finger. "That's it!" He grabbed Sarah's arm, squeezing it. "How serious is that?"

"Stop! You're hurting me. I—I don't know. I think it's different for different women. But from what I know it's a common condition during childbirth." She pulled out a phone and started searching online.

Livvie tugged on her mother's fingers. "Mama. Hugree."

Sarah squatted down to her daughter's eye level and ran a palm over the side of her face and back through her hair. "Didn't Kelvin feed you?"

Livvie nodded. "Apple sauce." She pronounced it "appaw soze."

Sarah stood up and took Livvie's hand. "I think I see some food machines over there. Let's go see."

When they were gone, Charlie slipped the pint from his pants and took a long drink.

C3 watched him. "You really need that now, Pop?"

Charlie stared at his son, his eyes flat. "Who're you to talk?"

"I was sober during Olivia's birth."

Charlie continued to look at his son. Finally, he said, "Have you ever thought about having her face fixed?"

C3 didn't answer for a long moment. "What?" he asked finally.

Charlie's tone was reasonable and persuasive. "Look, I'm sure you guys are doing all you can for her—taking advantage of whatever services are available. You know, so she can keep up."

C3 glared at his father. He said nothing.

"So … you want her to fit in, to be normal. It's what I would want. And yet—"

"And yet, what?" C3's voice was low with growing fury.

"I've just gotta say, son. She"—he shrugged—"looks like a retarded kid." He held out a palm. "There's things you can do about that. Why wouldn't you cover all your bases?"

C3's answer came out as a snarl. "Because your granddaughter isn't a base. And she's not a retarded kid."

"What do you mean—?"

"Excuse me! I'm not done!" C3 was yelling now. A security guard glanced in their direction. "Your granddaughter is a human being. She is Olivia Bernelli—Sarah's and my daughter. And she happens to have an extra chromosome, which means she has Down syndrome. And she is a beautiful child of God—just as she is."

"C, I'm just trying to—"

"Just as she is!"

A nurse came through a locked door and looked around. "Charles Bernelli?"

"Yes?" C3 and his father answered at once.

"You can come in now. Your wife's been stabilized."

Without looking at C3, Charlie rushed to follow the nurse back through the door.

Sarah and Livvie had returned from their candy machine odyssey. Livvie was waving a chocolate cookie that was missing a bite. Chocolate was smeared around her mouth.

"Chocat, Doddy. Chocat cooey!"

C3 lifted his daughter up and kissed her on the mouth, so that he now had a faint chocolate goatee. He took out his phone, opened the photo app, and reversed the image so that he and his daughter were looking at themselves. "Look, Livvie. We're twins!"

"Chocat, Doddy!" she cried, pointing and laughing. "Chocat, Doddy!"

"That's right. Chocolate Daddy." He lifted her up again and pressed his forehead to hers. "Ooh, I love my little girl sooo much!"

Livvie giggled and said, "Wuv you, Doddy!"

• • •

The text telling Greg about Ray Drucker had been from Wayne Holmes. The three of them, along with Keith Simmons, had been buddies back in the day.

Wayne had always frightened him. A powerful man in just about every way, Wayne was physically imposing and extremely strong, with enormous shoulders and arms from years of lifting heavy weights. Wayne had been a competitive weightlifter twenty years back, and while Greg didn't know if he was still competitive, he would have bet that Wayne kept in shape. Fighting shape.

Wayne was also a powerful man in the community. Once upon a time, he'd had aspirations to actually help people. Admirable aspirations. He'd been religious, and probably still was, if Greg had to guess. Wayne had always been a regular churchgoer, a devout believer in the Word of God, the Word of Jesus, which gave him moral authority. So when Wayne made a pronouncement about an event, or an individual, or about the way things ought to be, people listened.

He was a formidable and influential man.

But none of that was why Greg was now so afraid.

He was afraid because of what had happened to Keith Simmons five years ago. Keith had gone to the post office on a Monday morning. It had been raining hard, and not many people had been on the street.

As he came out of the post office, walked to his car, opened the door, and was about to get in, someone had exited another car—a white Chevy Malibu. The person, who wore a dark hooded sweatshirt, approached Keith, who seemed to recognize the person, who then shot him in the face, returned to the Malibu, and drove away. The only witness was 77-year-old Mildred Jenkins, who had also been at the post office and had been in front of Keith in line. Mildred had been delayed because she was filling out forms required to send a care package to her grandson, who was serving in Afghanistan. Once she had her package appropriately boxed, labeled, and paid for, she stepped outside, opened her umbrella, glanced at the sky, which was still dull with clouds, and turned toward her car.

That was when she noticed the quick interchange between the two people and the recognition on Keith's face. An exclamation of "Hey!" was followed by two quick pops, and Mildred witnessed the person in the hoodie whirl away from Keith Simmons, whose feet remained on the ground while his upper body folded onto the car seat.

Mildred was as tough as her grandson. She was not paralyzed by fear, but turned and went right back into the post office to report what she had seen. And yet, Keith Simmons's murder remained unsolved.

The memory of what had happened to Keith and the knowledge that his friend Ray Drucker had suffered an eerily similar fate had planted and watered a seed of terror in Greg's mind. And the fact that the information had been texted to him in such a matter-of-fact way made his anxiety seem all the more meaningful.

Keith had been a part of what they'd done and now Keith was dead.

Ray had been a part of what they'd done and now Ray was dead.

Wayne Holmes had texted that fact to Greg with the ease with which one might report the weather.

Everyone else who had been involved was dead, except for Huxley and Velosovich, and they were nowhere to be found.

Now it was just him and Wayne—unless one of the other two was after him. No—it had to be Wayne. He was the one with that combination of sneaky and take-charge attitude. He also had the stones to kill his own friends. And it had been Wayne who had goaded Ray on that night. Greg knew the way Wayne operated. Wayne was a man who eliminated obstacles.

Now only he and Wayne Holmes knew what they had done.

And Wayne was coming for him.

• • •

Dora and Missy learned that a dispute Katie Drucker thought worth looking into at her range involved Little Ru, whose real name was Clevon Paulson. His brother was Big Ru, real name Cleveland Paulson. The brothers were raised by their grandmother, Molly, who gave them their shared nickname because she was forever claiming that the brothers would "rue the day" they did whatever they had done on that particular occasion.

The Ru brothers had friends who lived on both sides of the law, but neither brother had ever been in any major trouble other than the occasional fight outside of Rudy's bar, a marijuana possession charge or two, and a handful of speeding tickets.

Little Ru and Dora were sitting at the counter at Rudy's bar, where Dora had ordered them both beers. She had asked to speak with Little Ru, who had suggested she buy him a beer to "lubricate his memory."

"So am I here due to your investigatin'?" Little Ru wanted to know. He had smooth, bronze-colored skin, and dark brown eyes that smiled happily along with his mouth. He was teasing her.

"Well, in a manner of speaking. I'm looking into what happened to Ray Drucker."

Little Ru's smile faded. "Yeah, I heard about that. Bad thing." He drew the word 'bad' out on the vowel.

"I understand you were involved in some kind of altercation with him at his range a while back."

Little Ru's eyes widened and he took a deep breath. "Well, I guess there's truth to that. I'll tell you to the best of my recollectin' what happened. I had my buddy Amos over—he lives in Amityville, and he brought his buddies, Elijah and Lincoln, along." Ru shook his head. "I don't know his friends, but I do know Amos, and I can say he's a good man. His friends," he shrugged. "I guess they're from Amityville too, but—" He shrugged again and left the rest of the sentence hanging. "I have a pistol permit and Amos had told those guys we were goin' to the range to shoot, so they brought pistols and we all went together, in separate cars. Anyways, we was going out to eat and to have a few beers later."

"No drinking before?" Dora asked.

Little Ru shook his head emphatically. "Nope. Can't drink before shooting. Them's the rules and I believe it's the law. They told us that a county permit is required to shoot a pistol at ranges in New York State, and Amos's friends, Elijah and Lincoln, had pistols but they didn't have the permit." Little Ru raised his eyebrows and tipped his head as if to say, "See what I mean?" He took several long gulps of beer, draining about half his glass, which he held up with an impressed look.

Dora drank a similar amount of her beer, politely keeping pace.

"So Ray's employee—boy name of Gabe Evans—wouldn't let them shoot. They had two options, he said. They could register their pistols at the desk, leave 'em there, then enter the range and shoot my licensed pistol or Amos's—"

"Amos had a pistol?"

"Yes."

"You didn't say that. It was licensed?"

"Yep, it was. The other option was to leave. Anyways, both his friends started yelling and cursing, so Gabe pressed a button that called Ray, who was in the office. Ray came out and explained the law—he said that this was not his range's rule. It was state law."

"Okay. What happened then?"

"The men got madder and madder until one of them, Elijah, pushed Gabe, who'd grabbed his arm and yelled, 'Ray!' Elijah swung at him, connecting with Gabe, then froze when he heard Ray rack his shotgun. He'd gone back into the office and come out with a twelve gauge, which he pointed at all four of us. He said, 'Time to leave.'"

Little Ru nodded, widened his eyes and tightened his lips for emphasis, then drained the rest of his beer. Dora drank hers, held up her glass, and nodded toward Little Ru, implicitly asking if she could buy him another. He shook his head.

"I tell you, Ray wasn't playing."

"So did you leave?" Dora asked.

"Well, Lincoln pulled his pistol, but at the same time, I put mines on the counter and put my hands up in the air. I wanted Ray to know I wasn't going to cause no trouble and I was hoping Amos and his friends would follow my lead. So I said, 'C'mon 'Lijah, Linc!' And they all listened. Ray nodded at me then. 'Time to go,' he said, a second time. So I looked at Amos and his friends and said, 'Let's go.'"

"And you all left?"

"I left, and the rest followed me. I waited at the door, and when Elijah got to the door he turned and said, 'This ain't over.'"

"What happened then?" Dora asked.

"Ray said, 'I say it is,' and everybody left. We all got in our cars and drove away."

"Do you think it was really over for them?"

"You mean do I think Elijah or Lincoln might have come back last week and killed Ray?" He shook his head. "Got to say I don't think so, but really, I don't know those guys—like I said. Seems like a lot of trouble for a little bit of pride, but some folks are like that. We all went for pizza from there and no one said anything, but … you never know."

• • •

"Get out!" Christine snarled at Charlie, who had been berating a nurse, shaking a finger in her face; he had been dissatisfied with her explanation of Christine's condition.

Now Charlie turned to Christine, his expression wounded and bewildered, like that of a hurt child.

"You can't be here and yell at the nurses!" Christine's anger vanished as a contraction hit, her eyes bulged, and a long, low moan escaped her mouth. The muscles in her neck were rigid as her head thrust forward in anguish.

The nurse clasped her hand. "Don't push. Don't! You're not ready."

Christine gasped as the pain withdrew, and she panted, glancing at Charlie. "He has to leave. Get C3 in here. He's in … lob- lobby."

The nurse looked at Charlie, who was now pouting, dejected—still the wounded, sullen child. "I'll go. I'll fetch my son."

As he left the room, the nurse gave Christine a searching look. "You don't want the father—?"

Christine shook her head violently. "Need someone who'll pray with me. C3's in recovery. He knows how to pray." Her mouth dropped open, her eyebrows flew up, and her muscles tensed as another contraction hit. Christine screamed.

Chapter 9

Dora walked into the John Farmer Club's bar early on the following Friday afternoon. A group of young men was at one of the tables; at another was a man of about forty-five in a gray herringbone jacket, a blue tie, a navy blue shirt, and black slacks. He was with a woman about ten years younger than he, who wore a smart black and white business suit and medium-height heels. She had layered, brown shoulder-length hair with gold highlights, and was nursing a vodka tonic with lime; he had a single malt scotch, neat.

Dora recognized the bartender as the same one who had been there a week earlier, when she, Missy, Adam, and Thelma had dined there.

She approached the bar. The bartender looked at her and raised his eyebrows.

She said, "Pint of beer—whatever's on tap."

"Blue Moon okay?"

"Great."

He brought her a pint and she sat and enjoyed the beer for a few minutes.

"Say—"

"Bart."

"Bart, thanks. I was wondering, have you ever seen a guy here by the name of Ray Drucker?"

Bart leaned forward, with his hands on the bar. He looked at Dora steadily. "The guy who got himself killed?"

"Why do you put it that way?"

"What way?"

"Got himself killed. Like he did something to bring it on."

Bart shrugged. "Just a figure of speech."

"So, have you?"

Bart let the question hang in the air.

"…seen Ray Drucker here?"

Bart shook his head. "Wouldn't know. He's just a name I saw on the news. Million guys come through here day to day, week to week, month to month. Some are members, some are guests. He might've been here. Might not."

"I see." Dora was enjoying the beer and was trying to decide whether to order another. "Who runs this place?"

"Depends what you mean. The whole John Farmer Club? The bar? The restaurant?"

"Let's start with the whole place."

The bartender looked at her for a long moment, then smiled and said, "Why don't you stop by Sunday afternoon? The owner has a get together for friends here every Sunday from three to five."

"Are you sure I'd be welcome? I'm not his friend."

The bartender's smile widened. "This guy—everyone's his friend. You'll see."

• • •

Victim number three was coming into focus. Of course, he was familiar from back when it happened, but knowing him and having the information I needed to take care of business were two different things.

Now I knew about his work—that he had the kind of job that could be done in an office or home. I knew he was required to be out of the house a lot, meeting with clients. He was reasonably well-to-do. His wife worked. I knew where she worked; I knew where they lived. I knew what he drove and what she drove. His schedule was somewhat unpredictable because of the kind of work he did. It depended on his clients' needs. He would not be hard to find. All he did was go to a gym, the supermarket, to buy gas, to meet with clients, to restaurants or take-out joints. Not much else.

My information sources had access to him and his family, and could get me my target's location on just about any given day, at just about any time. This was something we rehearsed often and regularly. I was in no hurry; I could bide my time. We've been at this for a very long while.

Meanwhile, I thought about killing him. I imagined killing him, and I pretended I had just killed him. The feeling of accomplishment that imagining his death brought me was powerful—almost enough that I wouldn't have to kill him.

Almost.

• • •

Adam had suggested revisiting Evergreen Drugs to see if someone there remembered Ray Drucker coming in to pick up his prescription on the night he was killed.

Saul, the same store manager they had spoken to about the video, was with a customer at the front of the store.

"I believe Fahira was here that night," he said.

"Fahira Long?" Dora asked, surprised.

"Well yes," the manager said. "You know her?"

Dora smiled. "She's a friend of mine."

He led the two investigators to the pharmacy at the back of the store, where Fahira and a young man were working.

"Fahira," Saul said, "these women are investigators. They'd like to ask you a few questions about last week's murder."

Fahira Long was dressed in a white collared blouse and brown slacks, over which she wore the store's green apron.

Dora grinned. "Look at you, looking all professional."

Fahira laughed. "Why, thank you!"

Missy spoke. "Saul tells us you were here the night Ray Drucker was murdered."

Fahira's smile was replaced by a sad grimace. "I was."

Missy asked. "Did you notice anything strange—either about the call that went out about his meds, or about his time in the store?"

Fahira shook her head and shrugged. "Like what?"

"Anything. Did he call about the prescription?"

Fahira shook her head. "I think it was a text—an automated text that's made by our system when a prescription is due to be filled and picked up. We also send robocalls. At the same time, we're alerted on this end, and we fill the prescription, so the person can come in and pick it up."

"And that's what happened with Drucker."

Fahira nodded. "It is."

"You're sure?" Dora asked.

"Oh, yes. The police were here and asked about it too."

"What about when he was here? Was he with anyone? Did anyone follow him around? Was someone waiting outside? Especially someone in a dark hoodie or hooded jacket?"

Fahira held her palms out. "I honestly don't remember. We see a lot of people every day, and it's been awhile, you know? And even with someone coming in today, I don't pay attention to what goes on with them when they're not at my counter, and I have no way, really, to see outside. I believe there are cameras for that."

Dora nodded. "We know."

"It was worth a try," Missy said.

• • •

On Sunday at 3 p.m., Dora and Missy walked up to the twin oak doors of the John Farmer Club. Unlike their previous visits, the doors were closed and locked. They looked at one another; Dora shrugged and pressed the buzzer.

"Yes?" came a man's muffled voice.

"Dora Ellison and Missy Winters. We're here to see the owner."

After a long pause, a buzzer sounded and there was a click as the door unlocked.

They walked across the foyer and into the bar, which was filled with young men and several scantily clad young women, whose suggestive body language implied a professional status of sorts.

The young men had athletic builds that were similar to those of the busboys and waiters Dora and Missy had seen at their previous visit to the club. Their European features were similar too in a general way, though Dora could not be sure that these were the same young men they had seen previously. Most of these men were not waiting on tables. To-day that function was served by scantily clad women.

The room's energy was focused toward a table, a dais of sorts, at the center of which an older man of perhaps sixty-five, with smooth ivory skin, was smoking a white, curved wooden pipe. Arrayed on either side of him were four other white men of approximately his age. One, Dora noticed, was the Beach City Savings Bank president Renny Lowell. The others included the mayor of a north shore town, an uber-successful real-tor, and a senior county commissioner.

The man with the white pipe wore an expensive-looking white suit jacket draped over his shoulders, like a cape. Men were queuing up to speak briefly with him, taking his hand, which was proffered fingers closed and palm down, offered as a king or pope might, to have his ring kissed. Though the man did wear a large gold ring set with diamonds and a sapphire at its center, the young men did not kiss his ring or bow. They took his hand, spoke to him, and were briefly answered in return. Both this older man and the younger man whose turn it was would incline their heads toward one another after their interaction, and the younger man would make room for the next man.

The older man spotted Dora and Missy and beckoned them over, holding up a hand for the line of young men to pause.

"Ladies! Welcome!"

They approached and Dora and Missy each briefly took his hand by the fingers as they had seen the young men do.

"I'm Don Christian. Welcome to my home."

"Thank you," said Dora. Missy said nothing.

"How may I serve you?" Don Christian asked.

"We're private investigators."

"With Geller Investigations." Don Christian nodded. He was smiling, his blue eyes amused. "You were just recently here with Adam and his office manager. How was your experience?"

"The food was delicious," Missy said.

"Wasn't it?" Don Christian said, proudly. "You had the duck?"

"Well … yes, I did," Missy's mouth was open in surprise. She clapped it closed.

"And you had …" He waggled a finger and squinted, concentrating, "Ah! Paccheri al Forno!"

"Yes!" Dora was impressed.

"And it was…"

"It was very good," Dora had to admit; she was finding Don Christian charming—and very likable. She forced herself to stop smiling and appear more serious. "You know so much, I suspect you know why we're here."

Don Christian raised an eyebrow. "I know you are investigating a murder." He held up a forefinger. "But I do not—know why you're here."

"What can you tell us about Ray Drucker?"

The man looked sad. He pressed his lips together and slowly shook his head. "Only what I've read in the newspapers, I'm afraid. Very, very sad. I feel for his wife and family."

Dora didn't answer right away, then asked, "Tell me about your club. You seem to attract a very … particular sort of individual."

Don Christian nodded, his eyes half closing, conceding the point. "Yes. We do. It's true. We attract young men who have come from … challenging beginnings. Homes where … how do you say … there is no home. Homes where the family is—" He rubbed the fingers of one hand together and then opened his hand, as though releasing its contents into the wind.

"Broken homes?" Missy ventured.

"Ah! Exactly! This is the perfect term. Broken homes!" He puffed on his pipe, which gave off a sweet smell that was not at all unpleasant. He exhaled and briefly closed his eyes. "We attract young men who have had trouble—who have come from these broken homes, who have never felt they belonged anywhere. Many have never felt loved. They have never been a part of anything. Can you imagine growing up missing the love of a family? The love of parents?"

He looked at them with real tears in his eyes.

"Actually," Dora said, "I can."

Don Christian nodded and looked intently back at her. "Yes, I believe you can. Well, you can imagine how valuable we are to these young men. With us, they learn discipline and they find love. They find a family."

"Love?" Dora mused.

"What about young women?" Missy asked.

Don Christian had been about to address Dora, but now he shrugged and looked at Missy. "For whatever reason, we attract young men." He glanced toward the ceiling. "These things are beyond our control."

"The young men I see here—they all appear to be of the same backgrounds," Dora observed.

Don Christian shrugged again. "Like attracts like. I can only hope that other young men—and women too—are lucky enough to find a welcoming environment, a family of their own, the equivalent of what we have created here—but among their own kind." He made a subtle motion with his head and a waitress appeared with two menus. "Please, allow me to offer you a drink and a meal. For two young women who help us by upholding the law and chasing criminals, it's the very least I can do."

Dora inclined her head, acknowledging the kindness in the way Don Christian acknowledged others. "I'm afraid we have other business to attend to, but thank you, Don Christian, for your courtesy and for your time."

Don Christian bowed his head, and Dora and Missy followed the waitress to the door.

As they exited the front foyer into the parking lot, a voice called to them. "Hey! Hey!"

A dark-skinned young woman in her mid-30s was standing just around the corner of the building, her head peeking around the side and into the parking lot area. "Hey! Come here!"

Dora and Missy walked over to where the woman, who was dressed in jeans, a dirty green T-shirt, and an equally dirty brown apron with wet splotches on the front, was standing. On her hands were rubber dish-washing gloves.

"Hey, you're the investigators, right?"

Dora nodded.

"Well, want to know the real deal about this club?"

Dora squinted and took a step toward the woman. "The real deal?"

"Let me tell you somethin', girl. This club like the Klan." She pointed a finger, first at Dora, then at Missy. "You check it out."

Dora opened her mouth to ask the woman to elaborate, but before she could speak, the woman glanced fearfully around and disappeared back around the corner.

Chapter 10

Sarah had been in constant contact with C3 for nearly 24 hours, as Christine struggled through a long and brutal labor with her *de facto* son-in-law as support and prayer partner. The decision was eventually made, and Christine reluctantly agreed, that she would have a C-section.

Now, finally, mother and seven-pound baby Lucas Pearsall-Bernelli were resting comfortably. The baby's father was allowed to meet his new son once he agreed to dispose of the liquor bottle one of the nurses noticed in the car and to behave himself. Christine joked with C3 that the new arrival was already more grown-up than his forty-plus-year-old father.

Relieved by the knowledge of Christine's and the baby's health and encouraged by the relative calm that had been restored to her work environment, Sarah was finally able to resume work.

"Read me the first paragraph," Sarah said to Lemieux, a slender, balding man with a black handlebar mustache. He was seated in front of a computer and she was standing and peering over his shoulder.

He nodded and his blue eyes scanned the words on his computer screen as he began to read with a hint of a French accent.

"Crime in Beach City is a complex and multifaceted phenomenon that has sources that span neighborhoods and socioeconomic demographics."

Sarah squinted over his shoulder at the screen, her arms folded across her chest, the fingers of her right hand tapping her left bicep. "When in doubt," she began.

"Trim it out," she and Lemieux said together. The phrase was her mantra, influenced by the poet and editor Ezra Pound, who had been a mentor to T.S. Eliot. While he was a Nazi sympathizer and had been charged with 19 counts of treason by the U.S. government, he had nevertheless influenced Sarah's editing style.

"Try this," Sarah suggested. "Crime in Beach City is complex, with sources that span neighborhoods and demographics."

"Got it," Lemieux agreed. "So the article would continue, 'Beach City crime resists generalizations. Many of our crimes are committed by individuals who have their own motivations and reasons. Nevertheless, statistics bear out that assaults most often occur in the area adjacent to the train station, where lighting is poor and individuals travel to or from New York City at all hours.' How is that?"

Sarah clenched her lower lip so that it protruded slightly. "I think it's okay for now. Go on."

Lemieux continued. "Poorer neighborhoods in Beach City lend themselves to crimes of opportunity that can enrich the perpetrators."

"Man, we've gotta be careful there," Sarah interrupted.

"I'm being careful," Lemieux protested.

"I hear that. Well, go on."

He did. "Police records show that disturbing the peace is often a problem at night in the summertime, especially around the hours when the bars close. Public urination and drunk and disorderly conduct tend to occur in similar circumstances."

Sarah nodded approvingly. "Good!"

"Here's where it gets interesting," Lemieux said. "You'll see what I mean. 'Statistics also demonstrate that racial tensions and crimes that flow from them have an associative if not causal relationship with organizations that are known to base their memberships on the racial makeup of their applicants, among other criteria.'" He looked over his shoulder at Sarah.

She looked back at him, her eyes moving quickly from one of his eyes to the other. The muscles around her mouth relaxed into a slow smile. "Sounds a little academic, but I like it. Maybe we can simplify?"

His eyes smiled with her. "Will do, and do we want to name some of these organizations?" he dared to ask.

"Not a chance," she said, her smile growing even wider. "They know who they are."

He nodded. "And so does everyone else."

• • •

The sky was a deep, cloudless cerulean and the air had been warmed by the afternoon sun. Dora had Freedom on a chain leash while Missy had Comfort on a retractable leash made of pink nylon ribbon.

"Comfort wouldn't like it if he knew you had him on a pink leash," Dora mused.

"Pretty sure dogs are color blind," Missy responded.

"Not the point," Dora said, slightly more severely.

Freedom walked slowly, calmly, regally—pausing to sniff here or there. She was serene—the queen of the neighborhood, and she knew it. She did not deign to dignify with even a glance the occasional dog that barked at her or strained against its leash for a sniff at her hindquarters.

Comfort, on the other hand, dashed madly in every direction, as though he had just remembered a bit of goldfish cracker the children belonging to the white Lincoln Navigator parked nearby had spilled by the curb over here. Or the bit of chicken bone that had spilled from the garbage yesterday on the lawn strip of the house over there. Or a tasty bird turd dropped by a seagull in the middle of the street that no other dog had yet gobbled up. He knew where all the best turds and goodies were. For such treats, Comfort had a mind like a steel trap—information he shared only with Freedom.

Their owners, Dora and Missy, meanwhile, were busy looking at the gardens people in the neighborhood were beginning to develop for the spring. Dora had little patience for gardening, but she enjoyed the results—the beauty and the smells of flowers, preferably lots of them.

Missy was the opposite; she had the patience for stopping to admire and sniff, for browsing at the flower and garden stores, for spending money on perennials and annuals that would enhance the ledges and countertops of their apartment. She loved the planting, feeding, and watering, the pruning and nurturing of the plants until they grew into healthy decorative specimens.

Both women enjoyed walking around the neighborhood with the dogs, appreciating what neighbors were doing with their gardens, laughing at their dogs' antics while keeping sharp eyes on whatever they might decide to eat.

"What did Katie Drucker say?" Missy asked. She knew Dora had called their client earlier, but had been listening to a podcast with headphones on, and hadn't overheard the conversation.

"She got hold of Ray's phone. She figured out his password two days after he was killed. She said it was easy—her birthday. She gave me five names and numbers, and made me promise not to tell anyone I spoke to that I was calling on her behalf, that she was our client, or that the numbers came from her."

Missy stopped walking and spread her palms wide. "Well, that's silly. What are we supposed to tell them? We don't tell them we're investigators? What are they going to think?"

"I didn't say we can't tell them we're investigators." Dora, her expression unchanged, glanced back at Missy. "Doesn't matter what they think. We just won't say any of those things."

"Well, who else would have hired us?"

"Hey"—Dora tipped her head, the precursor to annoyance—"replay what I just said. 'They can go ahead and think whatever they want.'" She enunciated slowly. "We don't have to say much—just give our bonafides and ask questions."

Missy started walking again. "So what are the names?"

"Wait 'til we get back. It's too nice a day to mess up with work—for at least twenty minutes, anyway." Dora took Missy's hand, and they continued their walk.

• • •

Back at the apartment, Dora and Missy sat together at the dining room table and examined the short list of names and phone numbers in their shared spreadsheet for the Drucker murder.

They looked up at the same time and at one another. "What do you think?" Missy asked.

"I think let's go see each one and find out what they know, and pay attention to their reactions to our questions. What do you say?"

"You're so confrontational," Missy mused, which made Dora laugh. Missy continued, "I say let's go a little more conservative. Let's research them first."

"Fair enough," Dora agreed.

Missy clicked a link to open her telephone database. "Now who are we looking for?" she asked.

Dora opened the Google Drive folder for the Drucker investigation on her phone and clicked on the "People" doc.

She read the names to Missy out loud. "Under 'Names from Katie Drucker' we have Wayne Holmes, Keith Simmons, Lewis Huxley, Micah Velosovich, and Greg Walker."

"My suggestion"—Missy began—"would be to collect what we can on each one before we start calling or going to see anyone."

"Agreed."

"So, the first was?"

"Wayne Holmes." Dora spelled the name out. She clicked a few keys. "Got his address. From there, I'll start with a basic Google search." She typed his name and address into the search field. "He's a realtor."

"Okay. Please log his info in, then let's go to the next name. We can start with basic info, then flesh out each one. The next name is Keith Simmons."

Missy typed his name into the telephone database. "I get nothing on the reverse lookup." She looked at Dora, eyebrows raised.

Dora looked back at her, thinking. "Skip trace DB?"

Missy nodded and opened a window to Geller Investigations' skip trace database membership and logged in. "Got his last known address. How 'bout the SSDI next. Let's see if the guy's alive first."

Dora widened her eyes and nodded. "Okay."

She connected to the Social Security Death Index, typed in Keith Simmons and his last known address. "Ah," she said, sitting back. "Deceased."

"Now let's find out how." Dora chinned toward the screen.

"Yup." Missy sat forward and googled the name along with the word "death." Links to several news reports came up. "Well look at that! Murdered. Five years ago."

"Open the reports," Dora suggested. "Let's read them, and see if there's follow-up."

The news reports detailed the shooting death of Keith Simmons, who had been shot before entering his car. Interviews with the single eyewitness, his distraught wife, and a brother revealed no clues as to who killed him. Short subsequent news articles demonstrated that the police had also come up empty.

Dora was leaning toward the computer and drumming her fingers on the table. "Next is Lewis Huxley."

Missy began typing, looking at the screen, then typing some more. "Got his last known, but nothing on his job."

"Leave it for now. Let's move on. Micah Velosovich."

"Same as Huxley," Missy said, after a few moments of typing. "Got an address—the number we have—and no job."

Dora pursed her lips. "All right. Let's do the last one. Greg Walker."

"Found info for him. Owns a home and a business that services computer networks. Married, apparently. Can't tell about kids yet."

"Let's try to round out what we can for the two we're missing info on and see what we can do to connect the Drucker and…?"

"Simmons."

"Simmons murders."

Chapter 11

Greg Walker was thinking hard while pacing around his home office. Theo and Sue would both be home soon, so he would have to try to temper the outward expression of his anxiety, and perhaps, his drinking. He peered from behind a corner of the curtain toward the street in front of his house, looking for … looking for what? He had not seen Wayne Holmes for years and did not know what he drove—probably a Mercedes or a Beamer, but how could he know for sure? Besides, Wayne was smart enough and rich enough to hire someone else to do his dirty work.

So what could he do to protect himself?

He went back to his desk, his peanut M&Ms and his tall vodka tonic, grabbed a handful of candy, and washed it down. Immediately, he began pacing again.

Maybe he could move. He could go into hiding. Go on the run. On the lam! He laughed out loud, then sighed, and the sigh came out as more of a moan. His local roots were too deep. His long-term clients— Sue's school and their church, both of whose networks he managed— could not function properly without him. He had a wife, a son, and clients whose business he badly needed for him to keep up with his mortgage and bills. He also had significant credit card debt.

Much better to be well-armed and fortified by his sugar and a few good stiff drinks before he faced whatever was in store for him. He went to the closet, opened his gun safe, and checked the 9mm Beretta 92Xi

SAO Luger and the tiny 12-round Canik Mete MC9. He checked the latter's magazine, then slipped the Canik into his pants pocket and returned to the window.

A light gray BMW M340i was driving slowly along the street. He removed the Canik from his pocket and held it flat against his thigh. The car seemed to slow as it passed his house, and Greg forced his body to relax. The car was exactly the sort that Wayne would own—flashy, expensive, and brand new.

The beamer drove slowly past and disappeared around the corner. Greg remained motionless and vigilant, waiting for it to reappear on a second pass. It did not.

After several minutes, he returned to his desk for more sugar and alcohol.

He realized he hadn't checked the shotguns today. He rushed upstairs, listening for Theo, who, hopefully, would call out, "Hey, Dad!" when he entered the house.

All his guns were new—bought at a show in Vegas, replacing models he'd bought from Ray years before.

The 28 gauge Benelli Super Black Eagle was under his bed, ready, should anyone break into the house while he, Sue, and Theo were asleep. He checked it, then hurried back downstairs to the coat closet, pushed the winter coats aside, and took out the CZ 712 semi-auto, his personal favorite. Loaded and ready. Wayne wouldn't get him without a helluva fight, and that's just what he was now prepared for—mentally and equipment-wise.

He sat down at his desk, grimaced at the recent photo of Sue and Theo, and opened a browser to Wayne's company's website. He stared at his former friend, thinking of the many meals their families had shared and the Sundays they had attended church together.

Wayne was perhaps the most avid churchgoer and the most dedicated Christian he knew. A true man of God. He would never forget the last conversation they'd had when he had said to Wayne, "What if heaven and God aren't real? What if we've made them up?" Wayne had said the strangest thing in reply. He'd said, "Well then, wouldn't we be all the more holy, that we'd created such holy ideas?" He wondered to what degree Wayne had repented what they'd done and if he thought murdering the guys he'd done it with was wrong. He suspected that Wayne had never considered the question. But, Greg wondered, what could the man's rationale possibly be? Well, the question would have to go unanswered, as intriguing as it was.

His thoughts shifted to the Wires, the Y.R.s—Young Racists—at the Club. They were so much more invested than he, Wayne, and the others had been. They utilized technology in ways he could never have imagined.

Most of his activity with the guys at the Club was banter at the bar, or occasionally, at other bars. As a group they had hassled young, lone Blacks, Asians, and Latinos—and maybe the occasional Jew—following them home from bars or stores. They'd driven around cursing and yelling at them, throwing beer bottles, and vandalizing their cars or homes. They'd had fun frightening the girls.

Until they'd finally gone too far. They'd known it, and they'd stayed away from one another and from the fear and shame they'd be reminded of if and when they were to get together again.

Fun had, for the most part, been the extent of what they'd done. Fun. Most of it, except that one time. Harmless fun.

The Wires could now spread their message far and wide, especially with a techie among them. Back in the day, he'd been the techie—which did them little good with their low-tech means of attack. Now, the Wires could troll. They could follow their victims around virtually. They could easily find, identify and target snowflakes with their stupid woke messages. They could call them by the names they really were—those nastiest of names that weren't tolerated by polite society. And the Wires were protected by the First Amendment. They were protected by the podcasters, and by the hordes of people—most of them young men, but women too—who believed everything they believed. America for those who, like the Founding Fathers, were white Christians.

The Wires spread their message that the snowflakes, the BLMs, the Jews, the Asians, Latinos, and all the rest, were no longer safe. They advocated for the violence the un-Americans deserved.

And they were protected by a particular aspect of the First Amendment.

All the Wires did if some authority stuck their nose in was to say, "Just kidding!" And that would be the end of it. Their speech, their texts, their trolling, their "C" word for the women, their "N" word for the

Blacks, and certain choice epithets for Latinos and Jews—all of it was protected if you just said you were kidding.

Just kidding!

It was all a Lampoon. Not serious, the Wires claimed.

And yesterday was a Lampoon Day.

Yesterday the Wires put a meme out on social media showing men how to put their wives in their place if they got out of line. They'd found or made a little video somehow of a wife being punched in the gut. Don't leave a mark, they said.

And then they added, "We're just kidding, of course!" And that's how it was done. That's how they got past all of those woke critics. Just kidding!

But the message got through. Their listeners, viewers, readers—their audience knew they weren't kidding at all. Not. At. All.

And the fear they were instilling got through too, didn't it?

One day every month was set aside as Lampoon Day—a day when a special message, a special meme, was crafted and sent out, and the Wires all over the country, and all over the world, boosted it, then said "Just kidding! It was just a lampoon!"

What fun!

Now they were attracting fans from all over the country who wanted to join them. The Wires attracted them with hashtags so that multitudes of supporters could jump on the bandwagon and pile on their targets, who were college kids, professors, members of Congress, housewives, and single women. Their targets suddenly found hundreds, thousands of people trashing them, finding and giving out their addresses, their email addresses, their social media handles, their phone numbers, and their license plates.

Everywhere they went, the Wires and their followers would be on these snowflakes and wokes.

And when called to task, the Wires' response was simply, "It was a joke. Can't you take a joke? It's performance art. You just don't get it. Why are you so sensitive?"

Greg marveled at their creativity; he was, he thought, the Wires' biggest fan.

But with all of this wonderful activity, Greg still felt that something was missing. Even after a few drinks and several packs of his peanut M&Ms, his life was still somehow less than full. So he headed over to the Club, where everybody knew his name.

• • •

"What connects the Keith Simmons and Ray Drucker murders are two things," Missy explained. She had been researching particular aspects of local history but had been saving her findings until she and Dora could discuss the connection between the two murders.

Dora widened her eyes and nodded, waiting.

"The M.O. is one. Despite being years apart, both were shootings that were more or less in public. The shooter was hooded and approached the victim, who was inside, or in Simmons's case, about to get into a car. The victim, who appeared to know the shooter in both cases, was shot in the face."

"Which could be a commentary related to motive," Dora said. "To erase who this person was, in a sense. The victim's identity."

"Not all criminologists agree with that sort of psychological profiling," Missy said.

"No?"

"The face or head is the most readily available target when your victim is in a car. And if the victim recognizes the killer or is responding to the approach, his or her face will likely be facing the murderer. This sort of disfigurement could also be an indicator of rage."

Dora grunted her agreement. She understood rage. "Well, according to the news reports, Simmons was not actually in his car when he was shot in the face."

"True," Missy admitted, then continued. "The other similarity is that both victims are part of a group of acquaintances. And, according to Katie Drucker, all of these guys apparently frequented the John Farmer Club."

"Interesting," Dora said.

"And speaking of the John Farmer Club. I did a little digging and learned some things about the place." She paused, but Dora said nothing. "It's old, first of all. Nearly a hundred and fifty years old. Originally the Tanberry Club, it started as an all-white club in response to the influx of Black people to that part of the north shore in the decades following the Civil War. It was one of the primary meeting places of the Klan, which lynched at least three local Black leaders they referred to as agitators, who, as they put it, 'wouldn't listen to reason.'"

"Jeez," Dora breathed. "The Klan on the North Shore of Long Island."

"In 1965, during the Selma to Montgomery civil rights marches, the club, which had changed its name to the John Farmer Club after its president at the time, had on its board local realtors, bankers, and other influential businessmen, who heavily influenced the politics of the vicinity."

"Nice," was all Dora said.

"Their leaders included Sylvester Wright, now deceased, a bank president and an Imperial Wizard of the Klan in the 1950s, prior to Farmer. Wright's son Seth, a bank vice president, and Kyle Lowell were also heavily involved."

"I know that name," Dora interrupted.

"I thought you might. He was the president of the Beach City Savings Bank. He's deceased, but his son, Renny Lowell, is the current bank president."

"Lowell was present when we were there."

Missy sat back in her chair. "Right, but these people don't broadcast their membership."

"And they're still a meeting place for the Klan?"

Missy tipped her head to one side and raised her eyebrows. "I don't know how active the Klan is these days, but they're apparently a descendent of sorts."

• • •

The plan I worked out with my helpers was turning out to be delicious, but complicated. People's lives are complicated, aren't they? And we're talking about people's lives—not just our targets—and their families. We had to keep track of them all—not only keep track, but do it in writing. And we each had jobs to do. Probably the hardest part was awareness. We had to be constantly aware, all of the time. And we had to be absolutely sure we remained undetected. We could not afford for anyone to be suspicious of us.

Two of us were using our own cars with our own license plates—risky, I know. We thought that would be okay, at first, anyway. I was the one killing them, so I was the one who would have to change plates for each killing. We wanted to keep any illegal activities to a minimum to minimize risk. Make sense?

Number three was pretty set in his habits, with just a few variables. He went to work or worked from home, which was a variable. He went out for a few hours. Where he went was a variable. When he came home, he usually stayed home. Now and then he had to go out for work, but that usually lasted a couple of hours at most.

This next one would be an easy target and wouldn't require anywhere near the time and planning as the first one or two. But he was dangerous. We had figured that out. He was often armed, which was important, and a major risk.

Time, as usual, was on my side. I could take a day, a week, a month, a year, a decade. But I'd get them—I'd get them all. And I'd make sure every one of them knew who it was that was coming for them. And for just a second they'd be hit hard because they'd know what a terrible mistake they'd made.

• • •

Greg parked his car and started up the walk to his house. He saw that another batch of cables, routers, and modems had been delivered. He nodded to Johnny, the Dorex delivery guy, who had just left the packages.

"What's shakin'!" Johnny said, with his usual friendly smile. Greg appreciated his deliveries, both because he needed the supplies and because he needed goodwill from somewhere—anywhere.

He and Sue had grown apart. Early in their marriage, they had been inseparable. What times, they'd had! Such fun—traveling, partying, loving each other's company! What had changed? Was growing apart all there was to it? He had other priorities now. They had Theo, who had been a handful growing up. But the video games seemed to have stabilized their son, who was quieter and perhaps more engaged now. Greg knew that Theo interacted with his friends in the games, where they fought against and alongside one another. But who knew what else they were doing?

He was well-armed enough to be sure of himself, but still, he had been trying not to think about Wayne. Unfortunately, that had only led to persistent, intrusive thoughts about him.

He had gone over every other possibility in his mind. No one else connected to what they'd done was capable of killing Keith or Ray. No one in the so-called victim's circle was so capable. They were pathetic creatures. Barely human, all of them. Lacking the intelligence to put together a plan. Lacking the courage to execute a truly well-thought out strategy, complete with the necessary tactics and organizational skills. Lacking smarts, the wherewithal, and, frankly, the guts, to plan the deaths of successful businessmen of their stature.

Finally, Greg gave in. So it was Wayne.

If he was going to think about Wayne, he wasn't going to let his fears run the show. He was going to gather real information; he was going to learn what Wayne had been up to since they'd been in touch five years ago. And if Wayne had killed Keith and Ray, and was now zeroing in on him, well, Greg wasn't going to sit around and wait for it to happen. Maybe, just maybe, he'd get to Wayne first.

He sat down behind his computers and continued the research he'd begun the night before. He knew Wayne had been a realtor in Whitville, just a few miles north then seven exits east on the Southern Parkway. What he hadn't known was that now Wayne had his own company—Homes by Holmes. His wife Karen was a vocal member of the state assembly. Greg wasn't surprised he hadn't known this. He avoided the local newspapers, both the physical and online versions. They were all obsessed with woke ideas and obviously had little connection to real people with real jobs, who worked for a living. The forces behind the newspapers, and the government for that matter, were so far removed from real people, from firemen, policemen, and mailmen, that their newspapers, their TV news, their pronouncements couldn't help but show how out of touch they really were.

But Wayne understood, and, apparently, so did his wife, who had gotten herself elected and, Greg had to admit, was now making a name for herself, charging after some of the more woke and offensive members of the state government.

Greg noted that Wayne had kept his head down for the first eight or nine years of his career in real estate. One's political views and activities might offend a potential customer—buyer or seller. But Karen Holmes had, Greg saw, shed all pretense of political agnosticism. She was a full-throated supporter of what the woke media called the extreme right and what Greg and Wayne and the guys at the Club called patriots. She supported banning books that endorsed anything resembling an LGBTQ agenda; she supported banning abortion from conception forward; she supported gerrymandering and redistricting any and all locales that might vote otherwise, and challenging any elections that did the same.

Apparently, Greg realized, the couple was a team. He found several newspaper articles that singled out Homes by Holmes for "redlining"—refusing to show or sell homes to people of color, to same sex couples, or Jews. He and other realtors in his vicinity were behind Whitville remaining one hundred percent white, Anglo-Saxon, and Protestant.

Wayne responded to the interview by saying he loved Whitville and had no control over who did or did not live there. He said he suspected that people who were not white probably preferred to live elsewhere, and he accused the newspapers, who had sent couples of color to try—and fail—to buy homes in Whitville of politicizing the real estate business in the vicinity.

Greg couldn't argue with any of it. Prior to her burgeoning political career, Karen had, until recently, stayed home and bought items at flea markets and resold them on eBay. They were a good looking couple.

As an avid churchgoer, Wayne was a vocal advocate for forgiveness. Greg snorted at the memory of Wayne's exhortations on the subject. The guy was a murderer and was now trying to kill him! He returned to his gun safe, removed both handguns and closed the safe, spinning the combination dial, then stuffed the smaller of the two into his pants pocket and strapped on his holster and gun belt for the other. Then he changed his shirt in favor of an extra-large polo shirt, donned a light jacket, hurried out to his car, and headed toward Wayne's last known address.

Chapter 12

Sarah, C3, and Charlie were sitting together on one of the crescent sofas in Charlie and Christine's immense living room. Opposite them, on the other side of the crescent, Christine reclined in an oversized pink fleece sweatsuit, its drawstring open at the waist. She was resplendent—surrounded by pillows. Baby Lucas was cradled in her arms, his head against her right shoulder, her face bent to his. Every few moments, she showered him with wet kisses.

The padded table between the two crescents was festooned with baby supplies—disposable diapers, lotions, wipes, paper towels, several cloth diapers, a baby bottle, extra nipples, and formula. Next to the table was a chrome trash pail with a foot pedal.

Christine looked across the divide. "Hand me the bottle, C," she said, holding her left hand out. "It's time to feed you, Lukey—yes, it is!" She nuzzled his cheek and kissed his lips.

"I'll get it!" Charlie jumped up. Since being thrown out of the birthing room, he'd been eager to make amends. He had not had a drink all day.

Christine wordlessly accepted the bottle from his hands without looking at him.

"Can I hold him?" he asked deferentially.

"He needs to be fed," Christine answered, still not looking at him. "Maybe after." She touched the bottle's nipple to the baby's tiny pink lips, which parted, and he sucked greedily.

"Look at him go!" Charlie marveled. "Quite the drinker!"

Everyone looked at him with shared disapproval.

"Of milk!" he protested.

Sarah felt her phone burr, and she retrieved it from the pocket of her black yoga pants. She looked at the text. "Jesus," she breathed, then got up and walked quickly to the windows that overlooked the boardwalk and beach. She dialed Lemieux, who had sent the text. She spoke quietly for several minutes, then returned to the couch and sat down, a stunned expression on her face.

"An eighth-grade boy in the middle school just hung himself."

"What?" Christine exclaimed and tightened her grip on baby Lucas, who continued to enjoy his meal.

"Who was it?" Charlie asked.

"The police aren't saying yet," Sarah answered. "Lemieux is writing the story from recorded interviews with the principal and some students the stringer is sending in. They're trying to get an interview with the mother. Once I approve the story, Esther will put it out on the website and social media and send it out in a newsletter. As more information comes in, we'll post updates."

C3 was shaking his head, his expression pained. "Why? Why?" He was present under protest and at Sarah's insistence, as he was not speaking to his father.

Sarah looked at him with focused intensity. "We're going to find out."

•••

As Dora arrived at Geller Investigations, Thelma was on the phone in the front part of the office, her voice broadcasting every word at maximum decibel in a timbre that was somewhere between a goose's honk and a buzz saw.

"So, what you're saying is he hasn't pooped on any of his walks for the last three days?" A brief pause. "Well, he hasn't pooped at home in two days, so obviously something's wrong. No! Do not feed him! If he's stopped up you might be adding pressure to his colon."

Dora hurried past the office manager, who continued while holding up a hand to Dora in either a greeting or a "leave me alone" gesture.

"Just leave him be," Thelma said. "I'll come right home and take him to the vet." Another brief pause, then, "I've got to go home, ladies. PeeWee's stopped up, so I've gotta take him to the vet!" PeeWee was Thelma's pitbull, who was nine years old and nearly as temperamental as his owner.

"Okaaay," Missy said.

They heard the bells on the front door tinkle as Thelma left.

Dora and Missy had been researching for several days, and it was time for them to compare notes. Dora sat down at her desk, looked at Missy, and waited.

"I heard from my sister again."

Dora gave a grim nod. "Bai? How is your father?"

Missy sighed. "Seventy-five percent of the time he's fine. The rest of the time he could be drinking gasoline, for all anyone knows."

"Has your family figured out a get-together?"

Missy nodded. "Kind of—tentatively." She gestured toward her computer. "Let's go over this, and get back to that."

"Sure."

"First of all, Huxley seems to have disappeared," Missy said. "He's had no transactions, paid no bills, put out no garbage, and his mail's been piling up for over a week."

"How do you know about the garbage and mail?" Dora asked.

"I told his next door neighbor I'm a cousin, and I haven't been able to get in touch."

Dora nodded and raised her eyebrows. "I knocked on Velosovich's door and asked the guy who answered where he is. The guy said, and I quote: 'Back to Russia.'"

"Who was the guy? Did he ask why you were asking?" Missy wanted to know.

"Nope," Dora said. "He's renting the place."

"From Velosovich?"

Dora shook her head. "Here's where it gets interesting. I asked—he's renting from Wayne Holmes." She watched as Missy turned toward her computer screen, her brown hair trailing behind and settling along the nape of her neck. "Come here," Missy said. "Take a look at this."

Dora rolled her chair across the room and looked at Missy's computer screen. On it was Wayne Holmes's personal LinkedIn page.

"Not much there," Missy commented, the glow of her screen reflected as little diamonds in her eyes and pale blue on her cheeks.

Dora noted one of the few hyperlinks on his page. "Click to the company page," Dora suggested.

Missy did. The Homes by Holmes page was that of a typical, upscale, boutique real estate company, located in Whitville, Long Island, and serving one or two towns along each of its borders.

They scanned the page for several seconds.

"Okay, go back," Dora said, and Missy did.

"Save that information into his file."

Missy copied the information from the page into a Google Doc that was a sub-link within the Ray Drucker murder directory on the company's Google Drive. The existing information included only the name of his church congregation and his company office and contact details. "I have his address from the DMV and his college information. His graduating class has its own Facebook page." Missy paused, her fingers poised above her keyboard.

Dora's nostrils flared, something she did when she was thinking hard. She lifted her chin. "Try googling him, see what comes up."

Missy did so. Nothing at all besides the Homes by Holmes web page, individual home listings he represented or had previously sold, and his LinkedIn page came up. But what also came up were a half dozen links for Karen Holmes. "Huh," Dora said. "Go ahead and click on one."

The first was a link to her Facebook page, where they learned that Karen Holmes was a longtime avid thrift store shopper who resold items she bought on eBay. "And they're very active in their church," Missy noted.

"Or so they want people to believe," Dora said.

Missy nodded in agreement then added, "And most recently, she's a member of the state legislature." She Googled "Karen Holmes Whitville" and clicked a blue link to a newspaper article and they both began to read.

"Wow," Missy said, after a few minutes.

"Yeah, wow," Dora agreed.

Missy sat back and folded her arms. "So she completely changed everything she believed in when she ran for Congress?"

"Hard to tell what she believed in before," Dora said. "She didn't seem political at all—at least not publicly."

"Interesting," Missy said. "So she's jumped on the extremist train and hitched her campaign to the national crazies."

"And it seems to have gotten her elected," Dora noted.

Fifteen minutes later they drove up to an address courtesy of the reverse lookup database for Wayne and Karen Holmes. Dora knocked and, after a moment, Karen Holmes herself opened the inside door and squinted through the screen. She was blonde, slightly overweight, with pink cheeks and blue eyes. She wore jeans and a sky-blue blouse with a collar. "Can I help you?" She looked past Dora and Missy, up and down the street.

"Karen Holmes?" Dora began.

"Can I help you?" She looked at them suspiciously.

"We're looking into the death of Ray Drucker." Dora held out a card. Ms. Holmes glanced at it but did not open the door.

"And you've come here because…?"

"Your husband was a friend of his."

"So?"

"So we've been hired to look into his murder and—"

"Who hired you?"

"I cannot divulge that."

"I see." The woman's tone softened. "Well, if it was his wife—Katie's a friend—so if she hired you, I guess you're all right." She opened the door and stepped outside, onto the top step. "I'm not sure I can be of any help, though. Ray was a pretty popular guy. Had lots of friends … that's assuming his friends might know anything about … what happened."

"You don't think any do?"

Ms. Holmes shook her head. "I don't see why anyone would. Ray was a decent enough guy. People liked him. Nothing shady about him that I'm aware of."

"What about your husband? Might he have any more information than you do?"

"I doubt it. Wayne's pretty busy. You could try his office. He's usually there during the day unless he's showing a property. He doesn't do much of that himself, nowadays. He's usually training the younger people who do."

"Would anyone at the Club have any more information?"

The woman looked sharply at Dora, and her posture changed. A hip thrust out, her chin pulled back, her eyes dulled and one eyebrow came down over an eye. "What club would that be?"

The woman watched as Missy spoke up for the first time. "The one Wayne and Ray and Keith Simmons went to. Oh, and Micah Velosovich."

The woman didn't flinch. Only her eyes moved from Missy back to Dora.

"And Greg Walker—he goes there too," Dora added. "You know, the John Farmer Club?"

The woman squinted beyond Dora and Missy as if looking to see if anyone on the street might be watching their interaction. She shook her head. "Sorry. Can't help you." She turned away and closed the inside door behind her.

• • •

Greg had driven around for several hours after leaving Wayne's street. He was now sitting in his car in his driveway, thinking about Wayne. When the old crowd had been together at the Club or each other's homes or out at some bar, they had been on exactly the same page. They had all been dedicated to their shared vision of the way things ought to be. They shared ideas, used the same language, and supported their vision through shared action. Not the equivalent of what was being done now of course, but they'd done some things, and they'd done them as a group. And of course, they'd done one big—really big—thing. That was why the Club had always worked and continued to work. Strength in numbers, strength in shared vision, shared action. Teamwork, and dedication. And utter silence.

Even when they'd gone their separate ways, to their separate lives, there had never been any notion of betrayal. They were united and dedicated.

Greg had not changed and had not budged from their shared commitment. He was pretty sure that was true of Keith and Ray.

So what had happened to Wayne? Why would he think any of them were a threat? Did he think they would go to the police? Why would he think such a thing? Did he think that they might tell their wives what they had done? They knew one another well enough and had been through enough and were committed enough to have absolute faith in one another's discretion.

He could not fathom what had happened to Wayne.

He had bought several baseball caps, each with a different Major League team's logo. He wore a different one each day for his surveillance. Today he chose an old Cleveland Indians cap, in part because the logo had been phased out as a result of pressure from the woke media, in part because to him, the head and the feather looked rather like a fist with an extended middle finger.

He had bought several pairs of reading glasses, each with a different color frame, and removed the lenses. Today he chose brown plastic.

He had rented an innocuous car, a Ford Fiesta because he was certain Wayne knew what he drove. The Fiesta was small, American-made, and gray; it would blend in well.

He backed out of his driveway and headed toward Wayne's office. He was noting Wayne's daily routines. As he drove, he had a sudden fear that Wayne was not personally trying to kill him, nor had he personally murdered Keith or Ray. He had hired someone—had taken out a contract on each member of their little clique at the Club.

This meant that Wayne's hired gun could have watched all of his preparations, and could be watching him right now. Which meant he had been spinning his wheels. Wasting his time.

He broke out in a sweat as he left the onramp and increased speed into the flow of traffic.

Maybe a better plan would be to just keep driving. Run. Stop at his bank, withdraw a load of cash, and head west and south, into friendlier territory, where no one knew him.

He swallowed, fished around in his shirt pocket, and found one of his little white pills. Popped it in his mouth. Found another and did the same with it. Then he washed the bitter taste from his mouth with his water bottle, which was filled with vodka.

When he approached the left exit that would take him west and, eventually, off of Long Island, he kept driving, fortified … for now.

• • •

The boy's name was Amir Batwal, and both Katherine Marbury, the middle school principal, and his mother, whose name was Jinani, said he was a good student—straight As. He loved science, particularly botany, and had written a children's book about the flowers that grew around Beach City. He was also a computer nerd who frequented chatrooms and gaming platforms. He led several virtual lives after school, inhabiting different avatars on various platforms. He was a ninja warrior on one, tasked with saving the world by retrieving a bomb built by an evil sorcerer. He was a scientist in another, planting, nurturing, and growing forests, fruits, vegetables, and flowers that would thrive in specific environments. In a third he was a suave musician, performing before mobs of fans in a complex society populated with avatars representing real humans who may or may not have anything in common with their avatars.

It was in this last game that he had drawn the attention of a handful of influential gamers, possibly because of his Pakistani heritage, which was also the heritage of his avatar musician. His mother explained that he was proud of his heritage and incorporated his background into many aspects of his life. His dream was to one day return to Pakistan and reunite with his extended family, all of whom lived in a particular village.

One of the gamers, whose online name was Cream Cheese, commented with a particularly derisive hashtag that was trending among white supremacists.

Within two days, an avalanche of hatred targeted Amir's avatar. Two days after that Amir's first and last names, his address, email, and cell phone number had been spread throughout an international system of white nationalist message boards, particularly among a loosely organized group who called themselves "accelerationists." The group advocated extreme violence as a means of accelerating the collapse of modern society and was known to target gay bars, synagogues, minorities and their organizations, and anti-fascist groups. Online hate and, occasionally, physical violence, weapons, including homemade explosives and automatic weapons, were their primary tools. Their means of communication were almost entirely via chat groups and gaming platforms.

Within hours, Amir began receiving threats that extended to his family. He was told that if he did not kill himself, his parents and younger sister would be targeted with a car bomb within three days.

Early the following morning, his mother brought clothes she had washed, dried, and folded to Amir's room for him to wear to school, when she found him hanging, lifeless and blue, against the inside of his bedroom door, with a noose around his neck made from one end of a rolled-up sheet. Several feet away was a folding chair Amir had stood on as he tied the sheet around his neck. He had then kicked the chair away. He left no note.

Chapter 13

Sarah had been sent some of these details by Gary "Re" Morse, the obsessive-compulsive BCPD officer who often worked the front desk and handled communications and public relations for the local force. Morse's official title was "communications associate." The responsibilities of the once permanent position of communications officer and public relations director had been downgraded and delegated to Morse, the third individual to occupy the position since its inception following the drastic personnel cuts that were part of a city-wide government cost-cutting and restructuring effort in 2008.

Sarah received frequent memos from Morse. She knew enough to leave the gory details and any information that might jeopardize an ongoing investigation out of her articles. Her job was to accurately communicate the truth while remaining diplomatic and restrained, thereby satisfying the public, her advertisers, and her de facto mother-in-law who was also the mayor of Beach City.

She posted the first article about Amir's death Friday evening. It was now midafternoon on Saturday as she and C3 pulled into the parking lot of Charlie and Christine's building.

Livvie had fallen asleep in the car, as it was time for her nap. Car rides were wonderful sleep aids where Livvie was concerned. Sarah carefully unbuckled her daughter's car seat and lifted her into her arms. C3 carried the bag of Livvie's supplies.

Once they arrived at the penthouse, Sarah knocked quietly on the apartment door. Moments later, it was opened, and Charlie charged toward them gleefully shouting, "Olivia!"

Startled, Olivia opened her eyes, observed her wide-eyed grandfather yelling and reaching for her, and began to wail.

Sarah pushed past Charlie with C3 in tow. "Put the bag on the table," she ordered, and, once C3 placed the bag on the little wooden table in the foyer, she handed Livvie, who was still crying, to him and began rooting through the bag.

After a moment, she turned to C3. "We forgot her pacifier."

"Shit," he said. "I'll go for it. See if they have grapes." Livvie loved grapes, especially green ones, and Christine often kept a bunch in their refrigerator just for their granddaughter.

Charlie was still standing with his arms out, his mouth half open in a silly grin, still ready to take Livvie. He ignored C3. "Can I take her?" he asked Sarah.

"Can you get her to calm down?" Sarah asked. When Livvie cried, Charlie tended to handle her as one might an unexploded bomb.

"You betcha," Charlie guaranteed, and took Livvie from Sarah as C3 brushed past him, leaving the apartment.

"Back in a few," C3 said.

"No rush," Charlie said, and shrugged when Sarah glared at him.

Charlie lightly patted Livvie's back and gently bounced her up and down. "Paw-paw's here, Livvie. Yes, he is!"

He pointedly did not look at his son, who left the apartment without looking back.

• • •

It had taken him quite a while, but Greg eventually answered Wayne's original text. When Wayne had told him that Ray had been murdered and, as far as Greg was concerned, implied that he would be next, Greg had mulled over how to respond, then texted back several days later, "I heard." He wanted his answer to be as free of nuance as possible. He did not want to broach the subject of getting together and rehashing old times. No one had ever expressed any interest in doing that. They'd all leaped back into their lives without so much as a backward glance to forget what had happened, to forget what they'd done. And now, Wayne had set about ridding the world of witnesses.

Five years had elapsed between Keith's and Ray's murders. Greg wondered why that was. Was Wayne busy? Had something happened recently to draw the attention of the police to what they'd done? Certainly, a second murder was risky. So, why now? His mind turned the question over repeatedly, but he never settled on an answer.

He had decided to ignore the possibility that Wayne had a hired gun shadowing him. Better to show the person that he wasn't a pushover—that he was taking matters into his own hands. That he was onto Wayne's game and was responding with his own.

He was parked a block from Homes by Holmes, his Indians cap and glasses disguise in place. He waited.

At four thirty, Wayne's blue 2023 Porsche Cayenne exited the lot and headed east on Jericho Turnpike. Greg followed fifty yards behind, his cap pulled low over his eyes and watched Wayne pull into the lot of an upscale restaurant that specialized in northern Italian fare.

He pulled into the back of the lot, which was three-quarters full. He thought briefly about eating but the tension in his throat and stomach dismissed the idea for him. Saliva collected and ran down both sides of the inside of his mouth. He was too nervous to eat. Following Wayne both allayed his anxiety and increased it.

As he waited, his mind wandered to his memories. They were all gun aficionados, and all had significant disposable incomes. They had enjoyed shooting together at Ray's range, followed by raucous dinners and drinks—or, just drinks—at the Club or a handful of other venues.

Wayne insisted on maintaining a superior arsenal of weaponry, particularly semiautomatic handguns and rifles. He talked about hunting—tracking and stalking prey, toying with it, cornering it, and ultimately killing it.

Greg tried to remember if he had seen trophies of game at Wayne's house. He didn't think so, which didn't mean Wayne hadn't hunted. Not all hunters displayed their kills.

So was Wayne tracking him, stalking him, toying with him, and preparing to corner and kill him? The man certainly had motive, and Greg was not just a witness, he was a participant, and the murders of Keith and Ray, combined with what he knew first-hand about Wayne, made Greg's conclusion obvious.

He opened Google Drive on his phone and pressed the Google Sheet labeled "WH." He entered Wayne's current location and the time, as he had with each of Wayne's movements.

The question was, now that he was tracking Wayne, what should he do next?

• • •

After their visit to Karen Holmes, Dora and Missy had been to Homes by Holmes, looking for Wayne Holmes. The cold shoulder that greeted them at what ought to have been a polite front desk led Missy to suggest that Karen Holmes had phoned her husband's office to let them know the investigators were coming.

Dora and Missy had just finished dinner and Dora was on the floor of the living room with Freedom, playing a tug-the-sock game. Freedom had dug her teeth into the sock and was jerking her head back, growling, and yanking Dora forward. Dora was mimicking Freedom, pulling back on the sock and growling. Missy had cooked—spiced eggplant with tomato and mustard seeds—and Dora had cleaned up.

"I'd like to know more about the game Amir was playing when he was targeted," Missy said, as much to herself as to Dora. Since the boy's death, they had been talking about the devastation his family must be struggling with. They had also been piecing together the relationship between Amir's suicide, and Ray's and Keith Simmons's murders.

"Call Sarah," Dora suggested, as she snarled at Freedom, who snarled right back. "She wrote the *Chronicle* article and might have more information than she's printed. If she has the name of the game he was playing, she might not want to print it for liability reasons, but maybe she'll share it with us if we explain we need it for our investigation."

Missy's mouth twisted with regret. "I should have thought of that."

Dora laughed. "That's why I'm here—your backup brain."

"Do you happen to know her number?" Missy asked.

Dora rattled off the number as Comfort began barking frantically and trying to scramble up the side of Missy's chair with his front paws.

"No, no, no," Missy chastised, but Comfort kept barking and flinging himself at the chair.

"It's just a car out front," Missy explained to the dog. Her tone was calming and serene. "It's nothing. It's okay, baby." Finally, she picked the little dog up and sat him in her lap, where he instantly curled up and went to sleep. She took out her phone and pressed the link to Sarah's number, then held the phone to her ear. "Hi, Sarah. Missy Winters."

"Missy! How are you guys? And the dogs, of course."

"We're fine. The dogs are a little nuts at the moment—Comfort is, was anyway, but par for the course. How are you, C and Liv?"

"We're good. What's up?"

"Would you happen to have the name of the game Amir Batwal was playing when he was targeted?"

"I do, but what's this for?"

"An investigation. We won't use it publicly."

"Long as you don't. It's called *Everyone's In* and it's a combination of role-playing, battle, community, and sim game. It's got a bit of everything and can get really complex."

"Great," said Missy. "Do you happen to know the names of the guys who came after him?"

"Two, well their avatars, Cream Cheese and Polar Bear," Sarah explained. "That was in the article. If you discover others in your investigation, would you mind sharing them with me?"

"I will if it doesn't compromise the investigation."

"Fair enough."

After ending the call, Missy turned back to her computer and got to work.

• • •

Today was Lampoon Day—the day they'd all been waiting for. Instead of crowding around a single computer at a table in the Club's bar, the Wires had pushed two round tables together. Each man sat behind his own computer, with multiple windows open. Each inhabited his own avatar that matched his screen name in the game *Everyone's In,* the log-on screen of which was open on all of their screens, as were windows into several chat groups. They logged onto the game, and their avatars met at "the square," a centrally located area in front of town hall in "the City," the most populous locale in the game.

They looked at one another across the tops of their open laptops, the light from the screens glowing on their faces.

Polar Bear, aka Bruce Jameson, pressed his mouth shut and breathed noisily—his breathing, affected by his asthma and his weight, was audible even over the bar's hubbub.

Lampoon Day was a day of attacking unsuspecting players both within and outside of the game—especially those whose avatars or names implied they were immigrants, minorities, gay, transgender, Muslim, or Jewish.

But Bruce was frightened—taken aback by the fallout from their most recent attack, and Lampoon Day was always earmarked as an all-out balls-to-the-wall assault. He looked at the others. "The freakin' kid's dead," he said, his eyes fraught with meaning—a "come on, guys" look.

After a momentary silence, White Cloud, real name Lawrence Tilden, snorted. "All it means for us is, some kid couldn't handle an online game. Big deal."

Snowman, aka Russell Hope, was new and was participating on a trial basis. The others were all paying close attention to his actions. "How 'bout we focus on what we're here to do," he suggested.

Cream Cheese, aka Chris Lombardo, agreed. "Man's got a point. One less immigrant to steal your job at Chicken-4U—know what I mean?"

They often commiserated about their jobs and much of the rest of their lives being replaced by immigrants—a selling point when recruiting members to the Wires.

So they piled on, filling the game and the chats on multiple platforms with insults about Amir Batwal's weakness, and urging others to join in—and many did. The Wires had discovered long ago that people love piling on when blame is heaped on a person. Many people are just itching to follow a bully, though they would have used the word "leader" rather than "bully." Perhaps it's human nature.

But Lampoon Day was so much more than attacks on one person. It was a day to celebrate white superiority and creativity. The Wires challenged one another to dream up ever more creative attacks on their targets, and they voted on the creativity of one another's attacks and on their effectiveness based on the responses that came back at them, along with any protests coming from the public and/or any powers that be.

Their responses to criticisms were various forms of "Just kidding!" and "Can't you take a joke?"

At the end of the evening, as they stumbled to their cars for the challenging drunk drives home, they all agreed—this had been the best Lampoon Day yet!

• • •

C3 stepped off the elevator, approached his apartment door, and found it several inches open. He stood for a moment, staring at the knob, the door, and the slim space of his apartment that was visible from the hallway. He reached back in his memory, trying to call to mind a visual of either him or Sarah closing the door. They were mindful about closing and locking the apartment, so he was pretty sure it had been closed.

He leaned with one ear toward the opening into the apartment. He heard shuffling sounds coming from inside and wondered if there might have been some reason for the landlord or super to need access.

"Hello? Alexander?" He opened the door, stepped inside, and received a blow to the side of the head. He fell to the floor, aware of only the cracking, metallic sound made by a solid object hitting his head. He was also briefly aware of pain, which filled what little was left of his consciousness. His vision had gone faint, and his view of the living room floor was tinted red.

Then, for an instant, he saw the boot—big and brown and filling his vision—and then … nothing. He did not see nor feel the repeated kicks to his face and the side of his head, nor the final blow to his neck. He did not hear the urgently whispered exhortations to "finish up" and "let's go!" He was not aware of the ringing of his cell phone or the passage of some forty minutes before Sarah and Livvie arrived to see what was taking him so long.

When she found C3 on the floor, bleeding from the nose, mouth, and one ear, Sarah frantically called 911. Once the ambulance came, she explained she'd have to wait with her daughter until she could find someone to watch her. She then called Charlie and asked him to meet her at the hospital, then called Kelvin and Vanessa to see if one of them could pick Livvie up and watch her, but neither of them answered. Finally, she grabbed several juice boxes, put a few handfuls of Cheerios in a baggie, and carried Livvie and her bag back to the car. She then took off for the Beach City Medical Center.

• • •

Dora was jogging around the apartment, taking tiny steps, and Comfort was following her while Freedom lay on the living room floor, watching the action. Every ten seconds or so, Dora would suddenly stop, spin around and pretend to attack the little Yorkie, and Comfort would react by crouching, ready for play.

Meanwhile, Missy was at the computer, researching *Everyone's In,* the game in which Amir had been bullied and attacked and which was, the police hypothesized, the source of the leak of Amir's personal information, which led to the viral intimidation that preceded his suicide.

"How's that going?" Dora asked.

Missy sat back and folded her arms across her chest. "Well, we don't have Amir's login or password for the game, and we don't have his computer, so I can't say for sure, but the timing of the attacks coincides with a surge of reported online intimidation, bullying, and persecution that appears to have been coordinated."

Dora sat down next to Missy, while Comfort, thinking the game was continuing, leaped up on Dora's calves a few times before realizing the game was over and then trotted over to where Freedom lay and sat atop the bigger dog.

"Quite a lot of this groundswell of activity"—Missy went on—"is flowing from IP addresses in our area." She clicked on several screens that had been buried behind others. "Look at this … and this, and this."

Dora read the paragraphs of diatribes Missy indicated. They were racist, sexist, bigoted, antisemitic, xenophobic, hate-filled rants sprinkled with the most offensive words and phrases.

"Come on!" Dora exclaimed. "Who pays any attention to this nonsense?"

"Kids do—and news media. But it's the former that's the problem. They get attacked, and others pile on. People love to pile on—and … well, look at what happened to Amir."

Dora looked thoughtful. "Do you think you could get into that game —*Everyone's In*—and find the people who went after Amir?"

Missy navigated to the game and spent fifteen minutes clicking and applying information to fields in several third-party websites she brought up. "Okay," she said finally. "I'm in."

"Well, that was impressive," Dora said. "But you probably could have just created your own login and avatar."

Missy blushed. "I like showing off for you. And anyway, now I'm in, and I'm completely anonymous. I'm going to bring up the *Chronicle* article—I think they printed Amir's screen name." She clicked and typed until the article she referenced was in front of them "Yup," she said, and clicked and typed some more.

"Okay. I've got a few screen names and two IP addresses. The others—looks like they're masked. But let's check these screen names against some of the names on those tirade pages. Here we go. These two, anyway, are the same. And I'll bet the others here are the ones that are masked—though I can't prove that."

Dora didn't answer. She was thinking—and digesting what she was looking at.

"So, do we think that these people, if that's what you'd call them, not only went after Amir but were also involved in the Ray Drucker and Keith Simmons murders?"

Dora's eyes shifted from the screen to Missy. "On the one hand, we have no real basis to say so. On the other, where there's smoke…" Her phone vibrated. She took it out, looked at it, pressed the red button, and held it to her ear. "Sarah—what's up?" She listened and her face darkened.

"What?" Missy asked.

"C3's in the hospital. He was found unconscious in his apartment, which had been torn apart."

"How is he?" Missy asked.

"He was beaten into a coma."

Chapter 14

Sarah sat next to the hospital bed with Livvie in her lap. She had managed to read Livvie a story—her favorite, *Goodnight Moon.* The book was not only Livvie's favorite, but one she insisted her parents read to her over and over, every night. The book was a centerpiece of her bedtime routine.

Livvie looked over at her father, who was motionless in the bed beside them, tubes protruding from his wrist, while a ventilator mask covered the lower portion of his face. From the other side of the bed, machines beeped in overlapping rhythms and tones.

"Doddy's still sweepin'?" Livvie asked.

"Yes, he is," Sarah answered.

"Doddy's vewy, vewy tiyewd." The little girl's face was serious and frowning with concentration. "I read to him!" she announced.

"That's a great idea," Sarah said and she took Livvie's favorite book from the bag and held it open so that Livvie could look at it.

Livvie's eyes moved around the page as though she were reading. "And eveybody say, goodnight moon! Aww done! Go to seep now, doddy!"

Sarah smiled through her tears. "Good job, Livvie!"

"Doddy's seepin' now!"

"That's right."

The door opened and Charlie burst into the room, his eyes red with tears. He saw his son in his hospital gown, connected to the hospital machinery, and sank to his knees. "Oh, my God! Who did this to him? Who!" He rested his elbows on the bed and covered his face with his hands. Sarah laid a hand on his shoulder. Charlie turned to look at her. "What are the doctors saying? Who did this to him?"

Sarah shrugged. "The doctors aren't saying much. And I have no idea who did this. I found him in the apartment, out cold, the place trashed."

Charlie stood up, his devastation morphing into mounting rage. "Let me find someone!"

"No. No, stay with me. I need you here, Charlie."

Charlie looked around and pulled a green-cushioned chair closer to Sarah and sat down.

"How are Christine and Lucas?"

Charlie smiled. "They're good. Lucas is, anyway. Christine's—I think she might be regretting becoming a mother at her age."

"I doubt that."

Charlie's expression grew serious. "I'm a little worried she might have some of that partum depression thing."

"Post-partum depression. Make sure you keep the doctors in the loop. Part of the issue with any kind of depression is a person tends not to want to tell anyone about it. Make sure she does—make sure she talks about it—to doctors."

Charlie turned toward his son. "Right now, I'm more worried about Lucas's big brother." He looked at Sarah. "Give me a minute with him, okay?" He gave his granddaughter a kiss on the forehead. "Love you, Olivia."

"Wuv you, Paw-paw!"

"Come on." Sarah lifted Olivia off her knee and led her out of the room.

Charlie sank to his knees again next to the bed and grasped his son's hand. "I'm so sorry, C. You need to get better for me, okay? You need to wake up. But first, I really need you to understand how sorry I am."

• • •

Greg looked at his watch; Wayne had been in the bank for fifteen minutes. He had documented Wayne's activities for three days and had noticed that Wayne drove from his home to work from eight fifteen in the morning to eight forty, with little variation. He stayed at work until fifteen minutes past noon, when he went out. His routine at lunchtime varied, depending on whether he was picking up a sandwich to eat at the office, heading out to a bar or restaurant, or eating at home. He returned to work between one and one thirty in the afternoon and remained there until four-thirty. It was now twelve forty-five, and Wayne, as he was each Friday on his lunch break, was at the bank.

Wayne had parked in the bank lot just beyond a white Ford F150 near the back of the lot, so very little of his car was visible to Greg, but he had been able to see Wayne pull into the lot, then emerge from behind the white truck to walk into the bank.

Wayne finally exited the bank and walked toward his car. Greg's hand nervously went to his gun, which was secured in his holster, but the movement was only a nervous tic, born of his preoccupation with killing Wayne. If and when he did take Wayne out, he would probably not do so in broad daylight in a bank lot.

Greg watched as Wayne disappeared behind the truck and, he imagined, got into his car.

Greg imagined himself, as he often did, walking over and blowing Wayne away through his car window. As he was distracted by this thought, a blue Toyota Prius parked at the curb in front of the bank and a small figure in a dark green hooded sweatshirt got out, walked to the back of the parking lot, and disappeared behind the big white Ford truck.

Moments later, the figure returned and as Greg watched, stunned, got into the Prius and drove away.

For a moment, Greg was frozen. Did that person…? Was Wayne…?

In a fog, Greg got out of his car, for some odd reason making sure to close the car door quietly, and walked into the bank's parking lot and the space between Wayne's car and the white Ford truck. He could see that the driver's side window was shattered and when he stepped closer he saw that Wayne's head was turned toward him, a look of surprised recognition on his face. In his left cheek was a bleeding bullet hole.

• • •

Several minutes after three o'clock in the morning, Missy's phone vibrated.

Dora's lifelong PTSD, which had increased since her battle with Diana Moran, made sleeping difficult. She looked at her phone, saw it was dark, then saw the light emanating from Missy's phone on the opposite night table.

"Miss, your phone," Dora said.

Missy groaned and stirred but did not reach for the phone in time. It stopped ringing. As she settled back to sleep, the phone trilled again. This time she answered it.

"Hello?" She listened, then sat up quickly, and listened some more.

"What's up?" Dora raised herself onto one elbow, but Missy had gotten up and walked into the bathroom. She didn't return for forty minutes, by which time Dora had gone back to sleep, assuming that Missy would have alerted her to any emergency.

"Dor." Missy gave Dora's shoulder a shake. She turned on the lamp on her night table.

Dora opened her eyes.

"That was my sister, Bai. My father's getting worse."

Dora squinted at Missy, one arm shielding her eyes. "Is he still ripping pieces of paper up?"

"I don't know. But he brought his computer to the curb—the computer they use for the business. It's brand new. And he goes out walking at night and refuses to come home. My mother was following him, to try to keep him out of trouble, but she's exhausted the next day, so Bai's doing it now—which isn't much better."

"Is there anything we can do?" Dora asked. "What do you want to do? Do you want to go there?"

"Maybe. I don't know. My father's always been so strong—the center of the family."

Missy climbed back into bed, her head leaning against Dora's neck as Dora held her, stroking her shoulder with a firm yet gentle hand. They lay that way for several minutes.

"Bai's family, who are from Kunming in south-central China, kept their Chinese names," Missy explained in a soft voice, as though she were talking to herself. "Our family name is Dontian which means winter, so I took the last name Winters. My given name is actually Meihui—beautiful wisdom."

"It suits you perfectly," Dora whispered. She had heard these things before but knew that listening to Missy tell her again was comforting for Missy.

"We've had a lot of tragedy in my family—depression and suicides, especially during the Cultural Revolution, when the whole country was turned upside down and people with real careers lost their jobs to kids and had to write terrible confessions and read them in public."

"That sounds awful," Dora murmured. "Our families have a lot in common."

Missy nodded. "I know."

• • •

Greg was driving as fast as he dared, terrified that when the police arrived at the scene of Wayne's murder, they would find him there and arrest him for the crime—no matter that he had seen it committed. Would they listen to him? *Of course not!*

He wondered if the bank had outdoor cameras, and if they they covered the entire parking lot. He didn't know, so he shook the thought away.

He drove without thought or intention, without knowing where he was going or what he was going to do next. He was in an anxious panic, as the active part of his brain focused on not causing an accident, driving within the law, and keeping an eye out for police cars—particularly in his rear-view mirror.

The thinking part of his brain was cowering in a corner of his mind, frozen in place, unable to rouse itself and decide on any next steps. Finally, it whispered a single word.

Alcohol.

He arrived at his house, hurried past Theo, who was doing his homework at the kitchen table, opened his office door, rushed into his office, and shut the door behind him. He sat down heavily in his rolling black leather office chair, opened his bottom desk drawer, and took out a bottle of his favorite vodka, Crystal Head Pride—a multicolored bottle in the shape of a skull. He was inclined to swill directly from the bottle but now that he was in his office, his safe space, he had enough presence of mind to go to the kitchen for a glass and some ice. As he returned to his office, he heard the front door close as Sue returned home from work.

She was wearing a white blazer over a violet dress and was carrying a brown paper supermarket bag with a beige rope handle. "Hey," she said, as she headed for the kitchen, stopping to kiss the top of Theo's head.

"Hey," he responded and returned to his office to pour himself the first of what would be several vodkas. He was still breathing hard, more from fear than from exertion. As he poured the first of the cold liquid down his throat, he heard the doorbell ring. He closed his eyes and felt the welcome, relaxing warmth, as the ease and comfort of the drink spread from his middle outward. He sank into his chair as the muscles of his back and legs relaxed. He was aware that his legs were shaking.

The door to his office opened and Sue was standing there. He raised a scolding finger and was about to remind her that she was to always knock and wait for his response before entering his office. But she interrupted him.

"The police are here."

• • •

Everyone at the Club as well as the online presenters and attendees agreed that Lampoon Day had been an overwhelming success. Events and activities that focused on finding and attacking vulnerable minorities were followed by training and explanations as to why certain techniques were successful while others were not. New members taught new Wires some of the most popular tropes and memes used for the most popular racist attacks. The Wires aka YRs aka Young Racists were proud of their labels, proud to call themselves racists, and exceedingly honored to display the secret emblems that referred to their noble membership in the John Farmer Secret Young Racist Organization.

Thousands of trainees aka Wirees aka YReez, as they were called in the organization, had joined the Club during Lampoon Day, and eagerly participated in the Club After Party—referred to as the CAP. The party encouraged everyone to drink their favorite beer or whiskey and to sing along with the Club Leadership, led by Don Christian himself, a half dozen traditional minstrel songs that had been popular over a hundred years ago on plantations throughout the south—songs about darkies and coons and pickaninnies.

All in all, the events of Lampoon Day and its aftermath exceeded even the Club leadership's most optimistic expectations. All were gratified that so many Americans just loved Lampoon Day!

• • •

Sarah held C3's hand, which lay limply in her own. Her fingers stroked the area between his thumb and forefinger, while her mind drifted to what she was going to do next. She could hear voices from the hallway, but their words were unintelligible. She barely heard the Darth Vader whoosh of the ventilator or the beeping of monitors.

Her mind was on Livvie, who was with Kelvin Franklin, who had generously agreed to watch her along with Vanessa Burrell's two boys, Drew and Buster. Kelvin's day job experience, caring for kids with special needs at the Montgomery School, was a great comfort to Sarah.

She'd received a call from the Beach City Police Department suggesting she stop by to discuss the break-in at their apartment and the attack on C3. She bent over C3 and kissed him on the forehead, careful to avoid dislodging any tubes. Then she tiptoed out of his hospital room and took the elevator down to the hospital's ground floor.

Twenty minutes later she was in the large back room of the Beach City Police Department, seated beside two desks that were pushed together to face one another. Behind one desk was Detective Paul Ganderson, the lanky, rumpled, taciturn partner of the loquacious Detective Gerald Mallard, who wore a suit that appeared to be so expensive as to be out of place behind a detective's desk at a police station.

Mallard began by following Sarah's description of the crime with a question. "What were …?"

"Charles."

"What, ah, were Charles's actions immediately, ah, prior to the, er ah, attack?"

"We were visiting with friends."

"At your apartment?"

"No, we were at Christine Pearsall's and Charlie Bernelli's apartment."

Detective Mallard looked surprised. "You were visiting with the mayor?"

Sarah nodded. "Yes, she's more or less my mother-in-law, since Charlie is C3's father."

When Ganderson spoke, his pockmarked face remained impassive. "C3 is your husband."

"We're not married. He's my long-term boyfriend."

"You have a child together," Ganderson said, by way of confirmation.

Sarah nodded and continued. "We had just gotten to the apartment when we realized we had left Livvie's, our daughter's, pacifier at home, and C went back for it."

The detectives waited but Sarah had nothing more to say.

"So..." Mallard said, encouraging her to go on.

"So, when I didn't hear from him for an hour, I texted him, then called, and when I didn't hear back, I went back to our place and found him." Her features clenched, and tears squeezed from her eyes as she began to cry softly.

Mallard pushed a box of tissues in her direction. "Are you aware of any conflicts he might have had—anyone who was angry with your husband?"

"Boyfriend. No. Well, he works as a drug counselor, so there is sometimes friction that's a part of his work. The facility where he works also serves people with mental illness, so conflict sometimes comes with that territory. But nothing that would lead to…"

"What about you?" Mallard asked.

"Me?"

"Your apartment was ransacked. Maybe someone was, er ah, targeting you?"

Sarah nodded. "Yes. That's exactly what I think happened. They weren't targeting me personally, though, but as the editor of the *Chronicle.* My computer was smashed and some disks were missing. This was definitely an attack on the *Chronicle,* and given that I'd been writing a series of articles about crime that specifically mentioned sources of local crime, I suspect that had something to do with the motive for the attack. I think C just walked in on the people who were trashing my stuff."

Ganderson leaned forward, his elbows on his desk. "Can you be more specific? Can you speculate as to who might have been behind this, given what you just said?"

Sarah's mouth twisted as she thought about the question. "Well, I've only talked about neighborhoods and demographics—and I've always been careful to say that we must not generalize. Crime is not caused by any specific demographic group or people from any particular neighborhood, but there are some things, some places, and circumstances we can point to, like older high school kids who are out on weekend nights, carousing. Or some poorer neighborhoods where poverty or broken homes can be a factor, or some of the behavior around the John Farmer

Club which, sources have informed me, might have members who were involved in the Amir Batwal suicide."

"Tell us about that," Detective Mallard suggested.

Sarah looked back at the detective. "Has someone come forward to tell you about that?"

"Why don't you tell us?" It was more than a suggestion—a subtle command.

Sarah told the detectives about information Lemieux had just the previous day shared with her. He had been unable to secure an interview with the mother, but Amir's father had spoken to a younger sister of one of Amir's schoolmates and learned that some of the other students in his middle school class had been cyber-bullied by a group of online thugs with names like Polar Bear and Cream Cheese. They participated in the same online games Batwal frequented, and had bullied kids in their class who were in an LGBTQ club.

Chapter 15

Greg sat in his cell wondering what had just happened and what was going to happen next. The detectives had cuffed him, read him his rights, and charged him with the murders of Ray Drucker and Wayne Holmes.

Where had he been the night of November 3, 2018, they had asked. How in God's name was he supposed to remember where he'd been that night? Home, drinking, very likely. And he'd told them that. Did he have a gun? Sure, he did. That was his right—and yes, all his guns were registered.

What was the evidence against him? Didn't he have a right to know?

He was being held without bail. Sue had come to visit him and explained that she thought that bringing Theo to the jail to visit was a bad idea.

No one was telling him anything and it was driving him crazy. And, not having a drink for over 24 hours—so far—wasn't helping.

He was alone, frazzled, and confused. He'd spent years having no contact with the old crowd from the Club, though he still went there often. Those days had been terrific but had ended in a nightmare. Those days were over. Ever since Ray's murder, he'd been more and more frightened that he was next, and he'd been more and more sure that Wayne was hunting each of them down and eliminating anyone who'd been there all those years ago.

But now Wayne had been murdered too.

He'd been certain he was next, and he'd barricaded himself in the house with packets of candy and bottles of vodka. He'd stayed away from Sue—not that they'd had much to do with one another anyway these last few years. And he'd stayed away from Theo. Whatever his relationships with his family, he was sure as shit not going to drag them into this swamp his life had turned into. They were in the house, but he hoped that by being by himself all the time, he was limiting any risk to his family.

What about Micah and Lewis?

He'd been sure that Wayne was coming for him, but it was the police who finally did. What the hell was going on? How could anyone say he'd killed his friends when he'd been absolutely shocked to hear they were being murdered? Suspecting that these same, formerly good friends, best friends, might be out to get him had been devastating. Now he didn't know what to think.

He tried to imagine how anyone might have pinned the blame for Keith's and Ray's murders on him. Impossible!

On this, the third day, he'd finally learned something. The lawyer that Sue had found for him, the husband of one of the teachers she worked with—a balding criminal defense attorney who wore glasses and a brush mustache, named Lester Scofield—had reached out to the prosecutor who had huddled with a grand jury and decided that the evidence, circumstantial though it was, was enough to charge him.

What was the evidence? DNA at both the Drucker and Holmes crime scenes.

Greg protested that this was impossible. His DNA could not have been at the crime scenes because he had never been at the crime scenes.

What was this DNA evidence? His hairs, on the left lapels of both victims.

The arresting officer and prosecutor claimed that he must have leaned into the driver's side windows to speak to the victims before shooting them, or perhaps he had leaned in to bring his gun barrel close to the faces of the victims since both had powder burns on the left sides of their faces. Either way, the evidence led to only one conclusion.

The police had been to his home, of course, to collect his DNA and to confiscate his weapons. Rather than give them the combination to his gun safe, he gave it to Sue and instructed her to surrender the handguns.

Scofield explained to him that all of the murders, including that of Keith Simmons five years before, had been committed with the same weapon. The NIBN—National Integrated Ballistic Information Network—had confirmed that the slugs had been fired from the same gun.

The license plates of the shooters in each murder had been identified as having been stolen. He protested that neither the plates, the cars, nor the guns belonged to him and he urged Scofield to challenge the police on these issues. So far, Scofield seemed to have made no progress. He also wondered if the police had video from the bank of Wayne Holmes's murder—video that would exonerate him. He had mentioned this to Scofield and was frustrated that he still had no answer.

He had known that none of his handguns would prove to be the murder weapon, and yet, the fact that his DNA was at the scene of the two most recent killings had truly rattled him. Someone had to be setting him up. But who? Velosovich? Huxley? The two had vanished. Would his lawyer be willing to help track those guys with Greg in a jail cell?

• • •

Charlie opened the apartment door. "Welcome ladies. Come on in!"

He stepped aside, allowing Dora and Missy to step into the apartment.

Dora handed him the fragrant paper bag. "Vegetable lo mein, kung pao shrimp, egg foo young, General Tsao's chicken."

"And that's all for Christine!" He roared with laughter, then caught himself, wheeled, and carried the food back into the living room.

Dora and Missy followed. "Does he talk like that in front of her?" Missy whispered.

"Probably," Dora answered. "But not for very long—especially now."

Christine was on one of the crescent couches, a multicolored baby blanket over her left shoulder. She was holding Lucas against her with his face to the blanket, while lightly patting his back. Lucas glanced at them both and let out a long fart. Dora laughed as she and Missy sat down on the other couch while Charlie put the bag of food down on the table between the two couches and went to the kitchen for plates and silverware.

"Oh, look at him!" Missy said, reaching toward the baby.

Christine instantly swiveled away. "No, no! Don't touch him." She smiled apologetically. "Sorry, I'm a little germophobic."

Missy sat down beside Dora. "He is beautiful."

"Isn't he?" Christine said proudly. "Takes after his mom!" As if to punctuate the observation, Lucas gave a loud burp and spat a stream of semi-digested milk onto the blanket and his mother's neck and shoulders. She laughed. "That part, he gets from his dad."

Lucas gave a contented sigh and closed his eyes.

"I know, Lucas," Christine whispered. "I could use a nap too."

"How are you feeling?" Dora asked.

"Hungry! Always hungry. And tired!"

Charlie returned with plates and silverware and began opening cartons and dishing out food.

Christine thought for a moment, then said, "Also, worried."

"About what?" Missy asked.

"About C. About doing the right thing for my child. About doing a good job for my city, and getting back to being mayor."

"I'm sure you're doing a great job," Dora said.

"Oh, I am. But is it great *enough?*"

Charlie had finished doling out the food. "Trust me, honey. It'll never be good enough for our little dude."

Christine looked annoyed. "I wish you wouldn't call him that."

He looked amused. "Well, he is a dude. I've seen for myself—and quite the dude he is. Takes after his old man."

"And old, the old man is," Christine said, glaring at Charlie when he looked hurt. "Touché, old man."

"I've also gained a stupid amount of weight," Christine said, as she twirled lo mein around her fork.

"Well, I'd think that's natural," Dora said. "You've been eating for two."

"Still am," Christine added, hefting her breasts.

"What about you? How have you guys been?" Charlie asked.

"Busy," Dora said.

"Working a case?" Christine asked.

"Cas*es,*" Dora corrected.

Christine looked at Dora, thinking while she chewed. "Drucker and Holmes?"

Dora shrugged.

"You can't say," Christine stated.

"My family's having a get-together," Missy said, while everyone else was eating. "I'm going to get to see my parents and my sister and a bunch of cousins I haven't seen in a long time. Not to mention my father, who's been struggling."

"When's the last time you saw them?" Charlie asked.

"Why didn't I know this?" Dora demanded.

"Too long," Missy said to Charlie.

Dora looked into her lap. She appreciated that Missy would soon see her family but felt left out since she had none. She tried not to mention her feelings since she didn't want Missy to feel bad. She wanted to be a welcome part of every aspect of Missy's world, and that this significant segment was occurring without her being consulted or invited—and that it seemed to be unfolding right in front of her—was painful and struck her as rude and difficult to ignore. Missy was meticulous about being proper and polite. Rudeness was so unlike her. Dora chalked it up to a kind of family myopia—inability to see one's behavior when it came to family. Dora knew all about that.

Christine was watching them both while Charlie was oblivious. She took the blanket from her shoulder, folded it over the wet section, and lay Lucas on it, face up. He had fallen asleep.

"That's wonderful! Will Dora be invited?" Christine looked hard at Missy, who paused and turned to Dora.

"Of course, assuming you want to come. I'm sorry if I forgot to mention it. I thought I did, but with what's going on with my father—anyway, you'll be bored with all the Chinese being spoken. I hadn't thought—"

"No," said Dora, evenly. "I guess you hadn't."

"Aww, kids," Charlie said, realizing what was going on. "How 'bout I get you something to drink? Nothing a little alcohol won't cure. White wine, Missy? Beer, Dora?"

"Sure!" Missy said, a little too cheerfully.

"No, thanks," Dora said. "I'm driving."

"You're moping, is what you're doing," Charlie accused. "Have one damned beer!"

Christine glared at her husband. "Leave her alone. She's a grown woman!"

Charlie's phone rang. He put it to his ear. "Bernelli Group." He listened, then broke out in a grin and ended the call. "C3 woke up!"

• • •

Sarah was holding C3's hand while a nurse looked at the machines he was attached to. She held a light in front of his eyes and instructed him to follow it as she moved it from side to side. He was groggy.

Except for following the nurse's instructions, he had been looking at Sarah. "My damn head is killing me." He squinted around the room. "I'm in a hospital? What happened? Why am I here? Where's Livvie?"

"She's with Kelvin, Vanessa, and her boys," Sarah said softly. "You were attacked in our apartment. You went back—"

"To get the pacifier. Right, I remember." He closed his eyes. "But I don't remember driving there, or whatever happened after that. All of a sudden, I'm here."

"Someone attacked you. There's video from the building, but they were wearing masks. One of the police detectives says they have a print —one fingerprint. But we don't know if it matches anything."

"So—so I'm okay?" His eyes had half closed; he appeared about to doze off.

"You definitely have a concussion, and you were in a coma, but mostly they're thrilled you're conscious."

"Wait—what day is it?" His eyes opened again and moved around the room.

"Sunday the fifth."

"Whoa. Three days?"

"Four."

"Holy crap. Wait. So, they're giving me pain meds?"

"I believe they are."

"I don't think I should have—"

"They know you're in recovery and they'll stop them as soon as they can. You'll be on over-the-counters more or less right away. As soon as you can tolerate it."

"I can tolerate it. So, who do they think—oh, my freakin' head! Nurse? Nurse!"

Sarah touched his arm. "She'll be back soon. But first, let me—" She bent over him and kissed him gently on the lips. "So, I've decided to stop writing exposés about local crime."

"Wait, why?"

She swung an extended arm from one side to the other, palm up—a *voilà* gesture. "Look at you!"

"Um, no!"

"Um, yes! Charles—they could go after Livvie!"

"We'll take precautions. I'll buy a gun."

"No guns!"

"But you're a journalist. You've got to do your job!" C3 gesticulated emphatically, pulling on his IV line. "Oh, shit."

"See? I need to take care of my family before I take care of this city! And no guns!" Sarah clasped C3's wrist and brought it into his lap. He took her hand and wriggled it more deeply into his crotch, startling Sarah. "Well, I guess *you're* getting better!" she exclaimed, laughing.

"I'm fine. I want to go home. I want one of your bean, rice, and cheese casseroles!"

"You're going to need physical therapy."

"I need a meeting," he said emphatically.

"That's right," Sarah agreed. "You need a meeting."

• • •

Beach City Police Chief Terry Stalwell looked at Dora and Missy over the glinting gold of his eyeglass frames. Then he took the glasses off and lightly bit down on the end of one of the arms. Dora could see how dubious he was and how reluctant to discuss the subject Dora had asked him about.

"The Simmons case was five years ago," he said, stating what they all knew.

"And you were there, Chief." Dora enjoyed a special relationship with Chief Stalwell, as she had solved several Beach City murders that had occurred on his watch. In gratitude, he had invited her to join the BCPD, and Dora had taken him up on his offer, only to find after attending the academy that the life of a police officer was not for her. She was too independent, too resistant to authority according to some. Nevertheless, their mutual respect and admiration ran deep enough for Dora to approach the chief with out-of-the-ordinary requests that many would have called presumptuous.

"What else do you know about the case?" Stalwell asked, then smiled. "What else has Trask told you?" He was letting Dora know that he was aware that Lieutenant Catherine Trask had once again breached protocol and offered information to Dora that ought to have been kept behind the blue line. Trask, however, was so exemplary in every other way—a tough-as-nails, no-nonsense, savvy, even brilliant officer who occasionally made unfortunate decisions that her boss thought of as going rogue. Like carrying on an unrestrained, barely clandestine affair with one of his detectives. Usually, he determined that her choices were too harmless to warrant poking the hornets' nest that was his favorite lieutenant.

"We know very little about the case," Dora answered. "A guy named Keith Simmons was shot and killed in his car by persons unknown."

Stalwell had been leaning back in his black leather office chair, his legs crossed, arms folded across his chest. Now he sat forward and gave a barely perceptible nod. "There's not much more to tell. It was a Monday morning and he had just come out of a post office and was getting into the driver's seat of his car. All of this was caught on a camera mounted outside of the post office, only four blocks east of the drugstore lot where Drucker was killed."

"A bullet was retrieved," Dora said, confirming.

 A Divisive Storm

"Yes," said Chief Stalwell. "Nine millimeter. Ballistics and the NIB-IN database confirm that the bullet was in fact from the same Glock 19 as the Drucker and Holmes murders."

"DNA?"

The chief blinked and Dora could see his reluctance to respond; she thought she could see a bit of shining sweat break out on his bronze complexion. "We have DNA from the Drucker and Holmes murders. We've arrested one Greg Walker. These guys were part of the same crowd."

"They frequented the John Farmer Club—a great bunch of people."

Stalwell gave a rueful smile. "You've been busy." He sighed. "I don't much like them either, but that's beside the point."

"Did you know about these relationships before Drucker?" Missy asked.

Stalwell turned to Missy and studied her. Finally, he shook his head. "We had learned what we could about Simmons's friends, including Drucker, Holmes, Walker, a guy named Velosovich, another named Lewis Huxley, and Don Christian—the big cheese over there. We also knew about his work relationships and college buddies, friends from childhood…" He shrugged. "But we didn't have anything that pointed in a definitive direction."

Dora pressed her lips together and looked pointedly at the chief. "Everything I've heard about and personally witnessed suggests that some seriously racist shit is going down at the John Farmer Club."

Chief Stalwell held her gaze, his expression focused with a hint of sadness. "Was there a crime you wanted to report?"

Chapter 16

Dora had phoned Sue Walker and asked if she and Missy could visit. Sue agreed, so they were now seated in a bright, airy living room, opposite Sue, a woman with a wide face, full cheeks, and smallish eyes, whose brown hair was brushed behind her ears. Between them was a wooden coffee table on which she served coffee in small blue and white cups that sat on matching saucers. Dora drank her coffee but Missy did not. Dora noticed a tremor in the woman's hand as she drank her coffee.

"Do you work, Mrs. Walker?" Dora asked.

"Sue, please. I teach third grade at Beach City North Elementary. One of Greg's clients is the school system, which has been nice."

"What does he do for them?" Missy asked.

"He sets up and manages their computer network. His clients are local organizations and small businesses. Our church, Beach City Methodist, is another client."

"What do you make of the John Farmer Club?" Dora asked the question carefully, without inflection.

Sue looked down toward her lap; the tremor in her hand increased. "He's been a member there for years. For a while a bunch of us—well, including these guys he's accused of killing—" She briefly closed her eyes. "Which is just crazy!" She blinked. "Sorry. I'm guessing you're referencing the Club's reputation as prejudiced?"

Neither Dora nor Missy responded. They waited.

Sue's mouth twisted, equivocating. "Look, it's like the talk you see on some of these news shows—yeah, there's what you might call racist elements, but honestly, it's guys being guys. They're not serious. They goof around with each other. They talk some racist nonsense, but they trash each other too. It was the way they blew off steam. But they didn't really mean it. It was all a joke to them."

Dora nodded but said nothing.

Sue looked at the two investigators, her expression pleading. "We have a good life—had a good life. Greg's done some stupid things with those guys."

"Like what?" Dora asked.

"Mostly, they drank a lot."

"Did he drink a lot on his own too?" Missy asked.

Sue didn't answer right away, then nodded slowly. "Some, but so what? I don't really know what else they did as a group, because he wasn't home. But I know they were at that club and he often came home kind of buzzed—so I guess he drove drunk. Oh, and I also know they sometimes went to the range before they went drinking. You know, Ray and Katie owned a range, and before that a guy named Bannion owned it. They all loved their guns."

"We know," Dora said.

Sue put her coffee cup down on her saucer and clasped and un-clasped her hands in her lap. "Anyway, this place would be a mess the next day and Greg would sleep in. I kind of think they went to strippers too 'cause he would come home smelling like cheap perfume."

"Was there … another woman?" Dora asked.

"Nah," Sue said quickly, then paused and raised her eyebrows, and tightened her mouth. "At least I didn't want to think that. I still don't. We love each other and he's—he has clinically diagnosed anxiety. I don't think he could manage another woman. But I will say his interest in me—in our relationship—has fluctuated." Sue continued. "I guess I need to talk about that. When we went out and had drinks, we'd come home and he'd be rarin' to go, but when he was out with the guys and came home, sometimes—not always, but sometimes he wasn't interested, which was odd. I didn't want to think about that. I figured it was the alcohol, but I would have thought the opposite would be true."

Dora asked, "How are things going with the police?"

Sue's eyes teared. "The problem is he has no verifiable alibis—for either of these murders. He's so damned disorganized. Doesn't keep track of time. Doesn't keep track of anything! He spends nearly all his time alone, much of it on the computer. He used to hang out with Theo —played basketball in the driveway, went to the batting range." She looked forlorn. "But not anymore."

"Couldn't the police verify his whereabouts based on his computer activity?" Missy suggested.

Sue shrugged. "I don't know. It's possible. I think they're checking."

Missy asked, "Can you recall anything that might stand out around the time any of the men were killed?"

"The police asked that. Not that I can think of. Greg never said anything about anything. He's been keeping more and more to himself—a trend that's gone on for 15 years or more. His involvement with the Club was, once upon a time, an open, social, very nice membership years ago."

"What changed?" Dora asked.

"About sixteen or seventeen years ago, his involvement at the Club suddenly became secretive. So did his friendships. Before that, we socialized with the other couples; we went to the Club together. But then it became an all-male affair. I just assumed they were having strippers and maybe hookers, so I kind of looked the other way. You know… boys being boys." She looked off into the distance, her finger tapping on the table.

"What?" Dora asked.

"Back when he became secretive about the Club, Greg disappeared for a few days. He said he needed some space but"—She shook her head —"we weren't having problems, so I remember wondering why he would need space."

"And?" Missy asked.

Sue shrugged. "All I know is, he was gone for a few days, and then he came back, told me not to worry about it, and everything went back, more or less, to normal. What was I supposed to do? But he was more secretive after that."

"He was out of touch while he was gone?" Missy asked.

Sue nodded. "That was before we had iPhones, but we did have cellphones—the flip kind I think, and he didn't answer his. Afterward, he wouldn't comment. He said he just had to take a break and assured me it had nothing to do with me."

"How did you handle that?" Missy asked.

"What could I do? I love my husband. He changed, but I love him. I was lonely, so I visited chat rooms for wives whose husbands strayed, for women who were struggling with menopause, for women with diabetes, women with cancer—all sorts of chat rooms. The support and the kindness were helpful."

"And your relationship with him…" Dora left the question open-ended, hoping Sue would fill in the blank.

She did. "I used to try to interest him but eventually I gave up. His lack of interest in me wasn't exactly a turn-on." She twisted her mouth ruefully. "A lot of marriages must be like this."

"Do you think he's guilty?" Dora asked.

Sue looked at Dora with a scornful expression. "Greg couldn't kill anybody. A paper cut freaks him out."

Several minutes later, Dora and Missy were in the car and were about to pull away, when the front door to the Walker home opened and Sue hurried down the steps to the car and knocked on Dora's window.

"Please come back in. There's more."

Moments later, they were back inside. Dora wondered what Sue meant when she said, "All right. You can't tell this to the cops. It's hearsay, really—I just—couldn't tell you. But now I realize I *have* to tell you."

Dora and Missy had looked at one another, unspoken questions and concerns in their eyes.

"This all happened seventeen years ago," Sue explained. She poured fresh coffee for the three of them. It appeared that they would be there for a while. "Greg and his friends had been drinking."

"Which friends," Dora wanted to know.

"Ray, Keith, and Wayne. I think two other guys, maybe. Micah, I think, and Lewis something."

"Ray Drucker, Keith Simmons, Wayne Holmes, Micah Velosovich, and Lewis Huxley." Missy clarified.

Sue nodded. "Ray had just lost his job with the county."

"I thought he lost his job a year and a half ago," Missy said, as she scrolled through her "Ray Drucker" Google Doc on her phone.

Sue shook her head. "Different job. He was a building inspector for public housing. He'd been drinking on the job—he was a big drinker, Ray was, and it encroached on his work. He lost that job around fifteen years ago and, after a hearing, was demoted to filing clerk under the thumb of one of the toughest office managers at county. He lost that job a year and a half ago, or thereabouts, for similar reasons."

"Okay," Missy said, now understanding about Ray Drucker's jobs.

"The guys had been keeping Ray company and drinking. He was hurt and scared and angry. He'd been told that if he was lucky he might get a job as a clerk working for Linda Jordan, a heavyset Black woman and one tough lady. That's exactly what eventually happened and she's the one who would eventually fire him, or fire him first. He was fired from a second job by Earl Lincoln. How he lasted that long, I have no idea. Anyway, I heard this from Greg."

"Recently?" Dora asked.

Sue nodded. "He was terrified of going to jail and he figured that this mess and the murders have something to do with what I'm about to tell you. He kept it to himself, but now he's freaking out, so he confessed all of this to me."

"Go on," said Dora.

"Well, they started off drinking at the Club and they were pretty drunk and they got loud and Ray and Keith got nasty. They trashed some lady there as she was coming out of the ladies' room and one of them—Ray, I think; he was the instigator—was going into the men's. The lady complained and her husband went over to talk to Ray, who threw a punch. There's a strict no-fighting policy at the Club. That's one of the ways they've stayed open this long, despite all the rumors you hear about the place."

"The racist stuff," Dora said.

Sue nodded. "All of that's true, but it's just men being boys. Immature buffoonery."

"Well, it hurts people," Dora said, her voice rising, but Missy laid a hand on her forearm, suggesting restraint.

"Go on," Missy said.

"So they went to one of the bars downtown and kept drinking. They were good tippers, so the bars and bartenders were tolerant of their behavior. But eventually, one of the women there complained too, and the bartender asked them once to quiet down, and when they didn't, he asked them to leave."

She paused and looked down at the floor, then took a deep breath and continued. "Well, as they left the bar, they saw this girl, a Black girl, walk past the bar. She was very young and pretty and she seemed to, what's the word, flaunt herself, as she walked by. She had on these short daisy dukes, and she was … well put together."

"What'd they do?" Dora asked, with an angry glance at Missy.

"Nothing at first. They went to a 24-hour convenience store for beer. Then they saw her again, inside the store. They waited until she came out and I guess Ray said something, and she said something back just as the guys were getting into their car." She looked pleadingly at Dora and Missy. "They didn't mean anything. They were just drunken fools!"

"What'd they do?" Dora asked.

"Well, Keith was driving, Greg was next to him, Ray was in the back, behind Greg, and Wayne was next to Ray. That's why I'm not sure about the other guys. I don't think they could have been in the car—Greg told me who was. Maybe there was another car—I don't know."

"Okay," Missy said.

"Well, Ray jumped out and grabbed the girl—dragged her back into the car."

"Then, what?"

"They took her to the Clean Acres Motel."

Dora's gaze had hardened into a granite stare. "They forced her, you mean?"

Sue shrugged. "Greg didn't address that—just said they took her there."

"So, they raped her?" Missy said, halfway between a question and an accusation.

Sue sighed and shook her head, tight-lipped and tense. "She was provocatively dressed, and was showing herself off like she was better than them or something."

Dora nodded definitively, her face thrust toward Sue. "They raped her." She looked at Missy and stood. "Come on."

Once they were outside, Missy was chasing Dora, who was striding quickly toward the turbo, which was still parked in front of the Walker home. "Where are we going?"

"What time is it?" Dora wanted to know.

Missy looked at her watch. "Eight twenty-five."

"The John Farmer Club, to see if Belinda—remember Belinda?—is still there."

• • •

Theo Walker was sitting in an armchair in the den, wearing headphones and immersed in the game, *Everyone's In*. If asked, Theo would have said that more of his life was virtual than not—certainly the more important aspects. While he wouldn't have said he lived for games, he might have said he lived *in* them.

In *Everyone's In,* he had witnessed the attacks on Amir Batwal, but while horrified, he had said nothing. A lot went on in *Everyone's In,* and in many other virtual life gaming applications, that was extremely unfair, even dangerous. You had to protect yourself. You had to be careful. You had to be quiet and watchful. You had to lurk.

He knew the Wires—had known them since he was a child and they were teens when his father had taken him to the Club. He had gotten to know everyone there. Some of his father's friends had brought their children as well, and they had come to know one another. He had been friendly with Billy Simmons and Pavel Velosovich when they were all preschoolers.

He knew about the racism and, unlike his mother, he didn't think it was just "boys being boys." As a child, he had overheard conversations that had confused him. Later, when he knew better, what he heard had shocked him. He knew it was dangerous. He knew his father's and his father's friends' behavior was wrong.

And so, he began taping. He used his phone, taping what he heard around the house. He gamed on his phone, so it was out and around and turned on. No one would know the voice recording app was running. He also attached recording devices to the house phones and installed surreptitious recording software onto his father's cellphone. He even recorded what occurred in the game *Everyone's In* from his avatar's point of view.

He began searching the house in his spare time. He didn't know what he was looking for; he knew only that he lived amidst secrets, and he wanted to know more. He wanted to be in on the secrets. Eventually, he searched his parents' room, and his father's closet, where he'd found a scrapbook that included a 17-year-old newspaper article about an unsolved case.

When his parents were out, as they were now, he kept one side of the headphones slightly off his ear; his father often received network-related equipment and would not be happy if he was home but did not answer the door. He didn't like to wait for his equipment.

The doorbell rang, then rang again. Whoever was at the door was persistent and kept ringing, so Theo got up from his chair, peeked out from behind an edge of the living room blinds, saw that it was the Dorex delivery man, and opened the door.

"What's shakin'?" As usual, the delivery man wore a cheerful smile. He held an electronic clipboard in his left hand, and Theo automatically reached to sign it. That's when he saw the delivery man's right hand, which held a black handgun.

The man's smile never wavered. "Come on with me," he said, still cheerful. "Don't you worry. No one's going to hurt you. Just walk to my truck and get in the passenger side and sit right down there. And hey"—The grin broadened—"Don't do anything stupid."

His headphones still on, Theo walked down the front steps to the Dorex truck, with Johnny Ray barely a yard behind him, the gun in his right coat pocket. He got in and sat down. Rather than go around the truck to the driver's side and leave Theo momentarily alone, Johnny got in via the passenger's side and, keeping the gun trained on him, stepped past Theo and sat down in the driver's seat. He started the truck and drove away with the gun trained on Theo's left side.

Chapter 17

Belinda Jackson was in the coat room of the John Farmer Club. She had been taking coat checks, handing out coats, and accepting tips for twenty minutes—the busiest hour of most nights, at least on weekends. Many club members, especially the older and wealthier among them, wore sport jackets, even in the summertime. She and Josefina had cleared the tables in the dining room and bar and scraped the majority of food from the dishes and placed them, along with the cutlery, in the dishwasher. Barry, the head chef, had gone home as soon as dessert had been served. Felipe, the *sous chef*, had gone with him.

Belinda went to the kitchen, found a cloth napkin, took the folded tissues she'd been using for her collection out of her pocket, and, making sure no one else was around, folded them into the center of the cloth napkin. She then folded the napkin into a small square and inserted it into the back pocket of her jeans. She'd been doing this since she began working at the club sixteen years earlier, originally as an underage dish-washer.

The idea had been her brother's, and after thinking about it for a few days, she'd tried it. She had to have access to the coat room, so she was unable to try their idea out for the first year of her employment at the Club, but she'd used that time to figure out other strategies. She stole unwashed silverware and kept it in a shoebox in the closet. She also stole napkins and cigarette butts from tables. She kept everything in separate shoe boxes—also Johnny Ray's idea. His girlfriend, Fahira, served as a lookout and bodyguard. She supported everything they had done and were doing, and she had certain special skills that could come in handy, though they hadn't yet.

Johnny's job gave him occasional limited access to people's homes and he'd also stolen cups, napkins, and plastic cutlery, much of it from backyard barbecues. He went around to side gates or the backyards of people's homes, claimed to require a signature for delivery—whether or not he did—and would surreptitiously walk off with the items. He'd once stolen a sweater, and they'd thought about tossing it into one of the cars, but ultimately decided against it. One of the wives might speak up and claim, "That's not my sweater. What's it doing in my husband's car?" Belinda had advocated that using the sweater would throw shade on the husband, suggesting he was cheating, but they'd voted her down —two to one. Cheating husbands weren't what they were after.

He'd found the motherlode when he'd made sure a house was empty by casing the party in the backyard and then ringing the bell. He'd then gone inside and stolen a comb from a bathroom, along with hair from a drain in a wad of toilet paper. Goldmine!

•••

Dora and Missy waited until the cars had all left the John Farmer Club, then went in the back way. They found Belinda cleaning the countertops in the kitchen. She agreed to talk to them and said she would meet them out back after she washed the floors, which was her last job of the day. She washed her way to the back door, she said.

They waited a half hour, and another half hour, but Belinda did not emerge.

Dora went back inside, looked around, and came back out to Missy. "She's gone. Must have gone out the front."

Missy held up a finger. "Come on. Follow my lead." She went back inside through the kitchen, through the restaurant, and into the bar where Bart, the bartender was serving a handful of customers.

"Is the manager in?" Missy asked, producing her Geller Investigations business card.

"What's this about?" Bart asked, then said, "You look familiar." He looked at her more carefully, but Missy didn't give him time to think.

"We're working with the police on the Ray Drucker and Wayne Holmes murder investigations. They were both patrons here, right?"

Bart looked taken aback. "What if they were?"

Missy shook off the question. "Not a problem. What we do need and what the police need is the full name, address, and phone number of your employee—I believe her name is Belinda."

"Belinda Jackson?" Bart looked surprised. "Why would you need—"

"Do you have that information?" Missy asked brusquely. She was speaking quickly, authoritatively. "Time is of the essence!"

"Hang on." He lifted a small door in the bar and went into an office that was next to the coat check room. He returned moments later with a piece of paper. "You're sure the police need this?"

Missy nodded. "Call the BCPD and ask for Detective Gerald Mallard," she said, taking the paper. "He'll confirm. Thanks!" She hurried back out the way she and Dora had come.

Dora followed, unable to hide her grin. *Another of Missy's hidden talents!*

• • •

Dora and Missy stepped from the car into the sort of warm spring day that retains a faint hint of chilly, post-winter air. They made their way up the walk toward a small, faded blue cape with white trim, and matching second-floor windows showing basic, nearly closed blinds. With the wide first-floor bay window, also displaying closed blinds, the house had the appearance of a blue face outlined in white, with half-closed eyes and a laughing mouth sporting horizontal teeth. The siding was cedar shake, whose paint was peeling. The bare concrete foundation was mottled with green mold and long cracks that ran throughout like capillaries. An overgrown lawn, riddled with weeds, was bordered by a four-foot-high chain link fence. In the driveway sat a familiar-looking blue Toyota Prius. Further up the driveway was an ancient, rusted Ford Thunderbird that might have once been gold.

Dora and Missy walked up to the aluminum screen door and rang the bell. Hearing neither the bell nor any response, Dora unsuccessfully attempted to open the locked screen door to knock on the inner door. After a few tries, she gave up and knocked hard on the door's metal frame.

She was about to knock a second time when the inner door was opened by a tall, slim Black woman.

She and Dora looked at one another for a moment, then the woman turned away to listen to someone speaking to her from inside the house.

"Long?" Dora ventured. "I didn't expect—do you live here?"

Fahira Long unlocked the screen door and pushed it open enough for Dora to open it the rest of the way. She stepped back grinning, and allowed Dora to pass into the darkened living room.

As Dora and Missy stepped into the room, the inner door was slammed shut by Johnny Ray Jackson, who had been standing behind it, and Long kicked Missy in the stomach. Missy folded to the floor, saying only "Wuh!"

As Dora turned toward her, Long kicked her in the side of the head, knocking her to the floor. But Dora did not stay there. She had no time to wonder why Fahira Long was at the address she had for Belinda Jackson. She instantly reacted on instinct. Rather than try to get to her feet and leave herself vulnerable, she rolled toward Long's feet and managed to grab a foot before the lithe woman could slip away, and with her other leg, swept Long to the floor while maintaining her hold on the foot. Dora grasped Long's left leg against her body, wrapped her forearm around Long's lower leg, then twisted as hard as she could, breaking the woman's ankle. Long screamed.

Only then did she stand up and kick Long in the side of the head, putting her to sleep.

From the living room, a voice was screaming, "Shoot her, Johnny! Shoot her!"

To which a man's voice replied, "I don't know Bel—it's the same gun as…"

With a glance, Dora surveyed the dimly lit living room. In a frayed blue chair at the far end of the room sat a young man wearing headphones around his neck that did not appear to be attached to anything. The dark-skinned man she realized must be Johnny was standing opposite the door, in front of a breakfront that held framed photos, holding a Glock 19 on the young man. The look on his face told Dora that he was extremely reluctant to use it. Next to him stood a Black woman in her thirties she recognized from the Club and now knew was Belinda Jackson, dressed in gray sweats, her hair in long braids.

Johnny handed the gun to Belinda and said, "Watch him but please, try not to shoot him," nodding toward the young man with the headphones. "We done enough," he said, then stepped toward Dora, in a boxing stance, leading with a jab and aiming to follow the jab with a right cross. But Dora was a step ahead of him; she snapped a sidekick toward his knee, breaking his kneecap. Johnny screamed and went down, and Belinda screamed and knelt next to Johnny, cradling his head, and pressing her forehead to his. She quickly rose to her feet and aimed the gun first at the young man, then at Dora, then back at the young man.

All this took only seconds, as Long had come to, overcoming the pain and whatever effect the break must have had on her ability to use her left leg. Dora had already personally witnessed how tough the woman was. Standing on her broken leg, she grimaced and kicked—an upward-facing front kick, to Dora's face.

Dora covered her face with her forearms and caught the kick with one arm, instantly wrapping Long's right foot, much as she had her left, and twisted. This time the ankle did not break because Long spun with Dora's twist and landed, her right foot unharmed, on her back. Dora leaped onto her, raining ground-and-pound blows down on Long's face, breaking her nose and bouncing her head off the dirty carpet. Moments later, with Long unconscious, Dora stood. As she did, Belinda backed away, halfway into a kitchenette, so that she could swivel the gun from Dora to the young man and back again. All this time, the young man had not reacted. He watched without expression. Dora wondered who he was. She also carefully watched Belinda Jackson's trigger finger. The woman was in tears, looking from Johnny Ray to Fahira, to the young man with the headphones, and finally to Dora. A few feet from the doorway, Missy lay curled in fetal position, groaning and gasping.

"Think about it, Belinda. You're going to shoot me with the same gun that killed Keith Simmons, Ray Drucker, and Wayne Holmes?"

Belinda's expression froze and she refocused on Dora. Then her face crumpled and she was suddenly crying. "I don't want to … At least…" She sniffled and wiped her nose with the sleeve of her sweatshirt. "I never wanted to hurt anybody, 'cept those that did what they did to me. All's I ever wanted was justice! At least listen to what I have to say! Why we done what we done!"

Dora knelt beside Missy and cradled her head in the crook of her arm. "Put the gun down, Belinda," she said, as she lifted Missy's head into her lap. "This is over." She turned to the young man. "What's your name?"

"Theo Walker." His eyes were red-rimmed and wet; he had obviously been crying.

"You're Greg and Sue Walker's son."

Theo nodded.

Dora exhaled noisily, shaking her head. "What a fuckin' mess." She turned to Belinda. "Okay, go ahead, I'm listening. But this killing has to stop, and you've got to let this boy go. Say what you've got to say, but it ends here."

Belinda blinked a few times. She sat down next to the coffee table and crossed her legs. She lay the gun on a pile of magazines that was splayed on the table, then she took a few deep breaths, gathering herself. She spoke haltingly at first but settled and focused as she spoke.

"My mother was a beautiful woman and she cared so much for me and my little brother." She looked sadly at Johnny Ray, who was clutching his knee, grimacing, and moaning softly. "She worked at the local country club, where she cleaned the meeting rooms, the kitchen, the bathrooms. Back in the day, there was a small hotel—they called it an inn—and she cleaned the rooms there, changed towels, linen, and toiletries. She cleaned the toilets and she tried to ignore the men who came on to her—if that's what you wanted to call it."

"This was the John Farmer Club?" Dora asked her.

Panting with pain, Johnny Ray was trying to stand up.

"Don't," Dora warned, and he twisted his lips and sank back down again.

"I need a doctor. You broke my fuckin' leg," he said.

"You'll get a doctor soon. And she's not taking you," Dora said, meaning Belinda.

"Shit," said Long. She was awake now and blinking. "My head," she muttered and looked accusingly at Dora. "This my family, Ellison. Don't you know that?"

Dora looked right back at her. "Your family killed people, and you helped. You need to be accountable."

"Shiiit," said Long, but she didn't move.

"Back then," Belinda said, answering Dora's question, "it was the Tanberry Club, but yeah, my Mama didn't think I knew what she put up with. Men grabbing her, throwing her against walls, stickin' their tongues down her throat, callin' her nigger girl."

"Jeez," said Missy, who was still trying to catch her breath.

"Go on with your story," Dora said, glancing again at Fahira, who was trying to rise, shaking, to her feet. Her left ankle gave way, and she cried out and fell again to the floor.

Missy sat up and took out her phone. "I'm calling 911. These people need medical care."

Dora nodded, and Missy made the call and gave the operator the address. Dora turned back to Belinda. "I'm listening. And, by the way, I accept that she had to take a lot of crap from men. Women, and women of color especially, take a lot of crap from men and it's never justifiable. I'm sure at her job it was particularly bad. But please, go on."

Belinda wiped tears from both cheeks. "My mother had to take a bus, a train, and two more buses—in that order—to get to work. Her shift was nine hours, but with the travel, she was gone from six in the morning to nine-thirty most nights. She had us—she called us her babies, even when we were teenagers. Back when this happened, I was 15 years old, and Johnny was twelve. Everyone said I was naturally beautiful; I never wore makeup, or lipstick or nail polish." She managed a small, proud smile. "I didn't need it—didn't think about how I looked. I loved to read. I read everything. Books took me away from my situation."

"Where was your father?" Missy asked.

Belinda's face shuttered; her eyes went flat and she looked at Missy with an empty expression. "Wasn't around." She turned to Dora and her expression came alive again. "But I sure did love my little brother."

Johnny Ray, who was on his side, still clutching his knee to his chest, lifted his head with love in his eyes. "I love you too, Bel."

"And we both loved school, and we both minded our Mama."

"So, what happened?" Dora asked.

Belinda took a deep breath and exhaled shakily. "So I was fifteen, and I was watching Johnny Ray after school. I did that every day because Mama didn't get home 'til late." She looked at her brother with a crooked, pained smile.

"He was quiet and he loved to read. He also had this little construction toy, and he loved to build all kind of things with it—buildings, bridges, forts. It had strips of metal with holes every little bit, and screws with nuts that let him attach 'em together. There were these cute little fake strips of wood too, also with holes. He was working on building him his own li'l city." Her face lit up as she spoke, and her eyes drifted to her brother. Then her face fell and she continued.

"So Mama was at work, and it was 'round nine o'clock—time for us to have our chocolate chip cookies and milk. We called our routine chippies. It was time for our chippies." She started to giggle but caught herself. "Anyway, I noticed we were out of milk just after dinner. We'd had one of those dinners where you add meat to a little packet, and mix it up. I don't remember what they were called. I knew Johnny Ray would be upset, and not much upset him. He was a quiet child, but he loved him his chippies and could get loud and difficult if he didn't have 'em. So, I told him to stay put, that I was going out to get him his milk so we could have us our chippies. He was in front of the TV, glued to some show— the adventures of someone and someone. I don't remember the names. It wasn't much more than a five-minute walk, so I figured I'd be back in less than fifteen minutes. I had a key and Johnny Ray was locked in the house."

Her mouth twisted as she stopped and struggled to describe what happened next. "I had to walk past a bar, and a bunch of these thirty-year-old white dudes came out, and they was drunker than hell, and they started saying nasty things."

"What'd you do?" Dora asked.

"What'd I do? I walked faster. I went to the 24-hour store. I got my milk, and there was a line of people, so I had to wait. After a few minutes, here come these same drunk white assholes, and they're still saying shit. I didn't even look at them. I just minded my business and paid and got out of there."

"And then what?" Missy asked softly.

"Well, some of them was in the store, and some was in two cars, and a few got out of one car and stood in my way, so's I couldn't pass, and they was still saying shit—and it was even nastier. What they was going to do to me—scared me half to death! And then the rest of them came out of the store—I guess they was buying beer—and they got in their car and, and I tried to cross the street, but the ones in front of me wouldn't let me."

"What do you mean, they wouldn't let you."

"Every time I tried to step anywhere, they stepped in front of me. And one jumped out of a car and grabbed me and dragged me back into the car." Her eyes filled with tears as she spoke. "He dragged me in the back seat while another one held me down." Her tears overflowed and ran down her cheeks. "They lay on me and held me so I couldn't get up, and they closed the door and drove away. Then they turned up the radio so no one could hear me screaming, and drove me to the Clean Acres Motel. One of them went in and paid. The others, they threatened to kill me if I yelled or told anyone."

"What'd you say?" Dora asked.

Belinda drew her head back and raised her eyebrows, astonished by the question. "I didn't say anything. They was goin' to kill me!"

Chapter 18

Theo Walker understood the gaming and social media landscape as well as most people understood real life. For him, those landscapes were significant aspects of life. He literally lived in the gaming and social media multiverse, and he understood their benefits, chiefly that he could be whomever he chose with whatever attributes and powers he could dream up. He could use his personas and avatars to achieve whatever goals he chose, which typically were social. He was shy around real people when they were physically present. Those with whom he interacted online were real people too, only he wore a different skin around them, which freed him from his inhibitions. He also utilized games to explore aspects of himself. He "became" a great musician, a scholar, a dog trainer, a firefighter, a soldier, and while his virtual experiences were a far cry from real life experiences, they were, for him, nonetheless valid.

He also used his online life, particularly social media and Reddit, to learn—most often about other people. Their likes, dislikes, preferences, fears, hopes, and dreams.

He was so adept at online life that he was aware of danger before it reached him. He knew danger when he saw evidence of it—usually in the behavior of others or their avatars.

He knew about the Wires at the John Farmer Club. He knew about them online; he not only saw what they did to Amir Batwal, he recorded their behavior and discerned how to identify the individuals behind it.

His father had taken him to the Club when he was younger and he knew these people firsthand.

He had known for a long time that they had been engaged in online white supremacist behavior. For much of his life, he had never paid any attention to them because he did not believe they had anything to do with him. Until recently, he had thought it was none of his business, the way that some people played football or hockey, sports that did not interest him, and were none of his business.

Theo had always been a sensitive child; he had inherited his father's propensity for anxiety. Early on, he had picked up on his father's racist behavior, though none of it was online. He was sensitive to any sort of bullying by virtue of being a child and having to protect himself. Self-preservation required him to notice dangerous behavior, so when he saw his father behaving dangerously, he took notice and, eventually, took action.

• • •

"And then?" Missy asked Belinda.

"You know what happened," Belinda answered, anguish in her voice.

"They raped you," Missy said.

"They did."

"All of them?" Dora asked.

Belinda's expression changed—went from devastated to satisfied. "That's right. All of them."

Dora could see she was talking about the rape … and something else.

"What'd you do after that? Did you go to the police?" Missy asked.

"Huh! Bunch of white dudes and a poor Black girl. Who they gonna b'lieve?"

"Did you go?" Dora persisted.

"Not right away, but yeah. The cop in charge of the investigation, if you could call it that—guy named George Cobb—said I was okay—a few cuts and scratches."

Dora shook her head. "George Cobb," she muttered.

"You know him?" Belinda asked.

"Yeah, I know him. He's in jail. Did a nurse or a doctor examine you?"

Belinda shook her head. "Nope. Cobb said I was fine, and that was that."

Dora nodded back. "Go on."

Belinda nodded. "So I went downhill from that point on. My schoolwork went bad—and I loved school, but I couldn't take it any-more. I cut class, I wore too much makeup. I started drinking at home, sneaking bottles in, going out—staying out all night, running with fast boys. 'Ventually, started shooting speedballs, and Mama said she was gonna throw me out if I didn't clean up my act, and that's just what she did. I had nowhere to go, so I went to my Aunt Rosie's and stayed there.

Rosie helped me get a job at the supermarket and told me if I wanted to stay, I could, but I'd have to work and give 10% of my pay in rent and that would start in one week. And that's what I did. I also got me a night job. Oh, and I started going to meetings. And you know what, my life got a little bit better, but only so much…"

Belinda glanced toward her brother, who was panting and still clutching his knee. "My brother found them all—he swore he would— by asking around and doing computer research and joining some of their groups, where they'd bragged about what they done to me. Then he went to each one as their Dorex guy, and he found ways to get into their homes. He paid attention. His girlfriend, Fahira, got temp jobs near some of them—at Evergreen Drug and a pizza place by the post office down the street. The two of them have been collecting information for sixteen years."

"After he found them, did Johnny kill them?" Dora asked.

"Yeah," Johnny said softly.

Belinda shook her head at her brother. "No, Johnny. You not takin' my rap." She looked at Dora. "He found them. I killed them."

Outside, the sirens, which had been faint, grew louder as diffuse alternating red and blue lights strobed across the walls.

• • •

When the tone sounded, the doors opened, and Greg Walker shuffled to his spot in the visiting room. He found the investigator Dora Ellison seated on the other side of the hard, clear plastic divider. They looked at one another for a long moment before Dora said, "Well, you sent for me, and I'm here."

Greg said nothing at first. Finally, he nodded and said, "Sue said I could talk to you. She trusts you for some reason."

Dora said nothing.

Greg took a deep breath. "I didn't kill anyone."

"So you say," Dora responded.

"But I did…" His voice trailed off. "I wanted to tell you." He looked expectantly at Dora, but she didn't respond. He looked past her at the guard standing behind her and to her left. He'd been struggling for days with what he was about to say. He was terrified of being convicted of the murders he had been charged with, and driven by terror, the agony of false persecution, and insomnia, Greg had come to the brutal conclusion that he had to come clean about what he had done.

"We were out drinking. Ray Drucker had lost his job."

"And?" Dora asked.

He blinked and looked down and to one side. "I was with Ray, Wayne Holmes, Micah Velosovich, Lewis Huxley, and Keith Simmons."

"Okay. So you were drinking with friends. So?"

"And there was some conflict or other at the bar, so they threw us out, and as we were leaving, this girl walks by—really cute Black girl in short shorts and a blouse that was tied off just below her—anyway, she gives us this look like we were garbage and she was some sort of queen. I'll never forget that look."

Dora nodded impassively. "So, she looked at you?"

Greg nodded. "Like she was better than us."

"Then what'd you do?"

"We went to buy more beer, and there she was again, at the 24-hour package store. Like she was following us or something."

"But … she was there before you."

Greg thought about this. "Yeah, maybe she was. Not important."

"No?" Dora was looking hard at him.

"Anyway, before we knew it, she was in the back of our car."

"Huh, before you knew it," Dora echoed. "How'd she get there?"

Now Greg looked directly at her—emphatically. "I think she wanted to be there."

"Did she?" Dora was noncommittal; she looked angry.

"Maybe someone grabbed her and threw her in."

"Who?"

His eyes widened. "Wasn't me!" he said, quickly.

"I didn't say it was."

"Might've been Ray. We ended up at the Clean Acres Motel."

"Ended up? Like the car made the decision all by itself, and took you there."

Greg glared back at her. "Maybe she wanted to go."

"Do you know how old she was?"

He mumbled an answer.

"What was that?"

"Fifteen."

"Fifteen—and you think that was what she wanted? Because you six guys were so irresistible that—"

"Okay, so we took her there."

"Then what'd you do?"

"You know. Sue told you. She told me she told you."

"And now you're going to tell me."

"We…" His voice dropped to a whisper. "Raped her."

"All six of you raped a fifteen-year-old girl." Despite already knowing this, Dora's gaze hardened. "You fuck. Do you have any idea what that girl's life turned into after that?"

"And that was our fault?"

She nodded slowly. "Damn right, that was your fault." She sat back. "Know why she was out at the store that night?"

Greg's body had angled away; he was no longer looking at her. "No idea."

"She was buying milk for her little brother to have with his cookies before going to bed."

Dora sat back satisfied, then asked. "You told all this to the cops?"

Greg shook his head. "Not yet, but I will," he said, as he wondered whether he ought to tell his lawyer.

• • •

Two hours later, Greg Walker was brought to a much smaller room that was the same indeterminate color. Across from him was Lester Scofield, and he wasn't happy.

"Why would you tell them that? Are you crazy? You were supposed to say nothing without me present. Nothing! Do you know what you've done to yourself?"

Greg looked at his attorney. "I told them because I didn't kill anyone. I was being honest. I was telling the truth, and it was about time. That's what you're supposed to do."

Scofield wearily shook his head. "No, you're not supposed to just vomit out information to the police. You're supposed to listen to your attorney. My job is to help you navigate the legal system. I'm the expert here, not you. You've thrown yourself under the bus!"

"What bus?"

"The legal system. You've confessed to rape! Not only that—you've given them motive for the murder charges!"

"Yeah, well they've already got my DNA—which was planted, by the way. I have no idea how that happened. So, what difference does it make? I'm fucked no matter what! I told the truth, and the truth is, I didn't kill anyone. We had sex with this girl—which, by the way, was consensual, in my opinion."

Scofield was breathing angrily, audibly out his nose. "Good luck with that in court! Well, let me tell you why I'm here today, other than to call the foolishness of your rape confession to your attention. The DNA they have isn't going to stand up in court!"

Walker looked at his lawyer in wonder. "What?"

Scofield was shaking his head and brushing his mustache to either side. "You could have walked, you idiot! Let me tell you something about DNA evidence. This isn't TV. This isn't 'well, we've got DNA evidence so it's open and shut.' This is real life and in real life DNA evidence has to be collected properly and stored properly, and guess what? Your so-called DNA evidence had all kinds of other crap mixed in with your DNA, your hair—including other people's DNA. Skin particles, from what I understand—from Belinda Jackson, who, I suspect, was the person who planted the DNA in the first place!"

Greg Walker was energized. He thrust a finger toward his lawyer, his eyes bulging, a grin blossoming on his face. "I knew it!" He had a sudden epiphany. "She was the fuckin' coat-check! I'll bet she got my hair off my coat!" He was shaking his head. "Gotta be!"

Scofield was peering at Greg. "So, there's something here I don't understand. You raped this girl—"

"Stop saying that."

"Well, you did."

"Yeah, well, you can stop saying it!"

"Listen to me. So you did what you did, and the girl comes to work at the club—as a coat check or whatever, so she can collect your DNA. Wouldn't she be terrified to work at the club where this guy who raped her goes? And why didn't you recognize her? You must have seen her enough if she was the coat check girl."

Greg looked down, then back up at his attorney. "I did recognize her. I knew just who she was, and she knew who I was. And I told her if she opened her mouth, I'd kill her. But if she didn't, we could go on with our lives—and that's just what we did."

Scofield stared at his client. "Well," the lawyer said thoughtfully, "that DNA isn't going to prove you murdered anyone, so you just stuck yourself with a rape confession."

Chapter 19

Once the police had secured the scene and the EMS workers had attended to Fahira Long's broken ankle and Johnny Ray Jackson's broken kneecap, everyone except Theo Walker was arrested. Dora and Missy rode in the back of a squad car to the Beach City Police Station where they were separated and questioned about what had taken place at the home shared by Belinda Jackson, Johnny Ray Jackson, and his girlfriend, Fahira Long.

From the station, Dora called the lawyer Robert Bishop, who was probably the most highly regarded criminal attorney in Beach City as well as a friend with whom Dora and Missy had worked on prior cases. Bishop instructed her not to speak with anyone at the station until he arrived. Dora correctly assumed that Missy would also want Bishop's representation.

Once Bishop arrived, Dora explained to him what had occurred, and he talked her through what she would say to the arresting officers, which was essentially the truth. The two women had gone to Belinda's home to see what she knew about the murders and had been attacked by Fahira Long and Johnny Ray Jackson.

Belinda, Johnny Ray, and Long were to be charged with kidnapping in the second degree, and Johnny Ray Jackson was charged with criminal possession of a firearm and menacing in the second degree.

Based on evidence at the crime scene and the statements and injuries of the parties, Fahira Long was charged with third-degree assault, a misdemeanor, whereas Dora was charged with second-degree assault, a felony—the difference being the severity of injuries sustained. The police held everyone involved until they and the lawyers could sort out what had happened.

Since Dora had called the lawyer, Robert Bishop, who would represent them both, Missy called Charlie Bernelli, who arrived an hour later, and put up bail for both Dora and Missy. Missy's release was delayed because she had offered her phone as evidence. On the phone was a recording of Belinda Jackson confessing to the murders of Ray Drucker, Wayne Holmes, and Keith Simmons, and implicating her brother, Johnny Ray Jackson, and Fahira Long as accomplices.

That these men had raped Belinda when she was barely more than a child gave Dora pause. Her first impulse was to look the other way, to condone Jackson's murder of three of the men who had raped her. She had looked the other way at least once in the past and allowed a killer to go free, a decision she now regretted. While she well understood the vigilante impulse, which ran strong in her, she was developing a conscience—which left her with mixed feelings.

Missy, she knew, would want her to obey the law to the best of her ability. Her relationship with Missy was changing her, probably for the better.

The following day, based on testimony from Theo Walker, the charges against Dora were dropped. Clearly, she had been attacked but was defending herself, although she had suffered far less damage than her adversaries.

Dora also learned the next day that Greg Walker had confessed to raping Belinda Jackson. On the advice of his lawyer, Walker immediately recanted his confession but was nevertheless charged with first-degree rape, given the lack of a statute of limitations in the State of New York.

Belinda gave the police contact information for her mother, Brenda Jackson, who lived with her boyfriend at an over-55 community twenty minutes northeast of Beach City. She informed the police that immediately following her rape seventeen years earlier, she had given the underpants she had been wearing at the time to her mother, which had been her mother's idea. Together they had agreed that Belinda would not come forward at that time, but her mother would keep the underpants as possible evidence.

Within two weeks, the underwear was analyzed and Walker's DNA was found in dried semen.

"How long does DNA last?" Dora asked as she and Missy were driving to Charlie and Christine's apartment.

"I'm glad you asked," Missy said. "I did a little research. The DNA itself can last more or less forever, but whether it does or not depends on how it is collected and stored."

"And the police were able to lift DNA from a pair of 17-year-old underpants?"

Missy nodded. "There's a case of dried semen providing DNA after a hundred years."

"Really?"

Missy bobbed her head emphatically. "A complete genetic profile using an alternative light source, a PSA test, and autosomal and Y-chromosome short tandem repeats."

"Ohhh." Dora raised an eyebrow and glanced at Missy, who was looking out the car window through the rain. "I kind of suspected that."

Missy turned and stared at Dora, startled.

Dora burst out laughing, then turned pensive. "I hate to say it but I'm glad Belinda murdered those men."

Missy pressed her lips together and shook her head. "Dor—"

"Well, the fact that they were rapists … I do have mixed feelings. No one deserves to be murdered, but"—She held up a hand—"I'm glad I'm not in a position to decide. Just saying karma took care of them."

Missy shook her head. "Wasn't karma." She looked out through the rain that was running down the outside of the window. "I thought you were going to try to talk me into squashing the recording. I've seen you employ your own idea of justice—and I can't say I've entirely disagreed with you."

Dora was thoughtful. "Yeah, well, that was then. But letting Belinda Jackson get away with killing five guys, or four or three or whatever it was, just doesn't sit right with me. She needs to face the consequences even though I can see where she was coming from."

"Huh," Missy mused. "I'm impressed."

• • •

When Dora and Missy arrived at the apartment, they found Christine, Charlie, and Sarah around the dining room table. The baby, Lucas, was between his mother and father in a traveling booster seat decorated with polka-dotted jungle animals. Livvie was beside Sarah and was riveted to Lucas.

"Where's C3?" Dora asked.

No one answered until Sarah looked at Charlie. "He won't come if his father's here. Why? Because his father thinks Livvie should have surgery to change her appearance, so she won't appear, in his words, 'retarded.'"

Charlie shook his head and rolled his eyes. "For God's sake, I was kidding."

Christine gave him a long stern look. "You were not kidding, Charles." She turned to Dora and Missy. "I've explained to my erstwhile son-in-law that he does not have to respond to everything his father says."

"Well, maybe my son can forgive me for saying something stupid." He gave Christine a searching look. "You're big on forgiveness, or does that not apply to me?"

His wife's look softened. "It does, and I forgive you. But this is between you and your son. He feels things very intensely, and it's his daughter you insulted. He'll come around in his own time. Besides, he just came out of a coma and has a traumatic brain injury. Give him time to get his bearings."

"He's really overwhelmed," Sarah pointed out, then changed the subject. "Have you seen yesterday's *Chronicle*? The Crime Scene page, in particular?"

The paper was already spread out on the table. Dora and Missy bent over it.

"So the police found Lewis Huxley!" Dora exclaimed, looking at Sarah. "Where?"

"Out east. Had changed his name after the Drucker murder, but left some bank accounts in his name. When he used one of them, the police found him."

"So, he admits being in the car," Missy said, paraphrasing as she read. "And he claims he never touched Belinda and is confident any evidence will bear that out."

"Most importantly," Sarah added, "he corroborates the rape and the involvement of the rest of them."

"I guess the cops never found Velosovich," Dora said.

Sarah shook her head and nodded toward the newspaper. "Did you see our other news?"

Dora and Missy looked, then Dora turned to Sarah. "I knew they'd found a fingerprint at your apartment. This guy worked at the John Farmer Club?"

Sarah nodded. "As a busboy."

"And he confessed to assaulting C3? You just say here that he was charged."

Sarah tightened her mouth so that her lips were a thin line. "He wouldn't give up any other names, so assuming he doesn't, he'll face first-degree assault and the possibility of twenty-five years. This is his second offense, so he'll get a minimum of ten."

Dora was looking at Charlie, wondering what he was feeling. His son, who was so like him—emotional in every way, with a tendency toward addiction—had just come out of a coma caused by a violent assault in his own home, and was now not speaking to him.

Charlie saw her looking at him and, as if reading her thoughts, rose and went to the bar.

"Do you know if the police have the murder weapon?" Dora asked Sarah, then added, "Johnny Ray Jackson was using it to hold Theo Walker."

Sarah's eyes twinkled and she smiled. "They have it and I believe it's been identified as having been used in all three murders."

Dora exhaled, relieved that her say-so was not needed to convict Belinda Jackson, with whom she identified and for whom she had some sympathy. Missy's phone recording of Belinda's confession and the murder weapon, which was at Belinda's home, would be plenty to convict her, with Johnny Ray Jackson and Long as accomplices.

• • •

For Theo Walker, there were two major differences between the Wires and his father; one was that the Wires had bullied someone to death. He knew about that because he was there—virtually. And not only was he there, he had taped the goings-on within the game that led to Amir Batwal's suicide.

As far as he knew, his father had never killed anyone. The other difference for Theo between the Wires and his father was that his father was his father. Nevertheless, when he eventually learned of his father's confession to the rape of Belinda Jackson, he was stunned. His father was wrong, and his father had committed a horrendous criminal act, and yet, he was still his father, and Theo could not turn his father over to the police. He loved his father, despite his imperfections.

And he did not have to.

So when Theo left his home one sunny day as spring turned to summer, summoned an Uber, and brought his computer to the police station, it was the Wires, the Young Racists, he was there to discuss.

The man at the front desk wore a gold nameplate that read "Lt. G. Morse."

"I'm here," Theo began nervously, "because I have evidence related to the suicide of Amir Batwal."

Lieutenant Morse looked back at Theo for a long moment, then held up a finger. "Just a moment," he said and disappeared into the back room of the Beach City Police Station. Moments later, Detective Mallard appeared in the doorway to the station's front foyer.

"What's your name, young man?" he asked.

"Theo Walker."

The answer gave Mallard pause. "Would you be related to Gregory Walker?"

"He's my father, sir," Theo answered.

"I see. Well, come on back."

Once Theo presented his evidence with help from a computer tech to the Detective, the evidence was handed over to a grand jury. Since New York State had no laws that offered punishments for cyberbullying, one week later, charges of aggravated harassment were brought against Bruce Jameson, Lawrence Tilden, Chris Lombardo, and Russell Hope. Prosecutors attempted to charge the same four individuals with hate crimes but failed to do so. Instead, the four defendants were charged and convicted of stalking in the second degree, a class E felony, and each was sentenced to four years in prison.

Chapter 20

Dora sat on the sofa, waiting patiently for Missy to come out of the bathroom. When the bathroom door opened, Comfort began barking hysterically.

"What's up with you?" Missy wondered, in the little dog's direction.

Dora smiled. "He sometimes forgets you're here, then when you pop up, he has to greet you—even though you've been here all along."

Missy chuckled. "I think at least one of our dogs is having some senior moments, even though he's barely five years old."

"Come here." Dora patted a spot next to her on the sofa.

Missy sat.

"So, listen. You know I have PTSD, right?"

"I do—and if you need different medication—"

"No, that's not what this is about."

"Okay."

"This is about the things that give me PTSD." Dora paused, peering at Missy, to make sure she was being understood. "I don't get PTSD from getting kicked in the head or being physically attacked."

"But Moran," Missy began.

"Well, yeah. But that was an exception. That was a sick, crazy, bitch who—never mind her. Follow me, here."

"I'm following," Missy said, her eyes wide and expectant.

"I get PTSD from being left out, from someone who loves me shutting me out, hurting me—"

"Don't you think I know that?" Missy interrupted. "I know about your father."

"This isn't about my father. This is about you."

"Me?" Missy looked stunned and went silent.

"This is about your attention to your family. All these phone calls about your father, and I get that he's a handful, that he has dementia, and that your family needs you. I understand that, and of course, you should be there for them."

Missy nodded. "Good."

"Please just understand that you're all I have. I have no family."

"I know that. That's why—"

"Stop, Miss! I just need to talk here. I have no one—no one but you. So, when you're pulled away, even for something as understandable as a family crisis, it's painful for me. I completely get that you've gotta take care of that. I get that they're having a party so you can all get together to observe your father and make difficult decisions."

"That's not why—"

"Stop! Just listen, would you? I'm saying I understand. But I'm also asking you to understand that it's hard for me. To be understanding. To be kind about this. I made damn sure not to love anyone for a long time. And then Franny came along and she kind of nursed me back to sanity. And then ... wham! She was gone. But then you were there, and you never pushed it. You were nice and easy and ... there. So, when you're suddenly not there, it's painful. So, just be kind and understanding about that, is all I'm asking. Do what you've gotta do. Go where you've gotta go. But be kind, and be understanding."

"Okay. I will. I promise."

Comfort ambled over to where Missy was sitting, sat down at her feet, and rested his chin on her shoe. Freedom followed, walking around the other side of the coffee table, and rested her chin on Missy's knee.

Missy looked at Dora and chinned toward the dogs. "My therapists."

A buzzer sounded.

"Shit," Dora said. "They're here." She got up from the sofa, went to the apartment door, and pressed a button that would let their guests into the apartment building. Moments later, she opened the door to find C3, Sarah, and Livvie smiling back at her.

"Well, come on in!" Dora said, forcing herself to sound exuberant. She stood aside as C3, with a bandaged head and a cane for support, ventured inside, followed by Sarah, who led Livvie by the hand. Everyone trundled into the living room, where Missy had put out cheese, crackers, crudités, and cheese-flavored crackers for Livvie. Sarah had called ahead to request the latter.

"Hey!" Missy said, as their guests entered the living room. "Come in and sit down. We thought it was about time we had a party for a change. How're you feeling, C?"

C3 shrugged. "Pretty good, actually." He sat down in an armchair. The dogs went from guest to guest, sniffing.

"How is Livvie with dogs?" Dora asked.

"Watch," Sarah replied, as Freedom, whose head stood higher than Livvie's sniffed the little girl, who wrapped her arms around the big dog's neck and pressed her face to Freedom's. Comfort, not to be outdone, stood on his hind legs, his front paws just under Livvie's arms.

"Okay, then," Dora laughed.

Everyone but Livvie sat down, with Sarah and Dora on the couch, and Missy cross-legged on the floor.

"There's beer and wine in the fridge. Scotch for Charlie over on the shelf by the TV. Is Charlie coming?"

"C3's gotta take it easy and follow a traumatic brain injury protocol for a bit," Sarah said, changing the subject from Charlie.

"What's the protocol?" Dora asked.

"Rest, mostly," C3 answered, shrugging with a shy smile. "MRIs now and then. He needs to avoid looking at electronic screens, and bright lights. Oh, and they gave him anti-seizure medication."

"You have seizures?" Dora asked.

"It's preventive," Sarah replied, watching as the dogs made their way to C3, who hugged both dogs and grinned at his fiancée.

"A dog might be therapeutic," C3 suggested, to Sarah.

"Yeah? Who's walking him at 3 a.m.?"

"Me," C3 insisted.

"I'll believe it when I see it," Sarah said, with a dubious grin, then paused, equivocating. "Although … a service dog might be helpful with Livvie."

The buzzer sounded. "I'll get it." Dora got up and pressed the button for the downstairs door, then stood by the apartment door until a knock came from the other side. "Watch the dogs," she said, as she opened the door.

"Hey!" Charlie exclaimed and threw his arms around Dora.

"How 'bout letting your family in first," Christine chastised.

"Sorry." Charlie stepped back, an abashed look on his face, to allow Christine, who was holding little Lucas, to pass.

Charlie pecked Dora on the cheek and grinned. "What do you think of my accessory?" He nodded toward the enormous, birds-egg-blue baby bag slung over his shoulder.

"I think it suits you," Dora said mock seriously.

Dora guided Christine and Lucas to the sofa, next to Sarah and took a seat on the floor. Two dining room chairs completed the circle made by the couch and twin armchairs, with the coffee table in the center. Charlie hugged and kissed Sarah and Missy, then stopped in front of his son.

"You going to acknowledge me?" he asked.

"You going to tell me how to raise my daughter?" C3 responded, his face impassive.

Charlie hesitated. Everyone waited. "No," he said.

"Okay, then. Nice to see you, Pop," C3 said, with a chill remaining in his tone.

His father looked back at him for a long moment. "Okay, then." He turned to Dora. "Got scotch?"

Dora pointed to a shelf on their little breakfront, where a bottle of Dewar's White Label stood. "Just for you. Sorry, no single malt."

Charlie shrugged and grabbed the bottle. "Guess I gotta slum it." He headed for the kitchen in search of a glass and ice.

Christine sat Lucas next to her against a couch cushion. "I explained to this one"—She nodded toward C3—"and his father about forgiveness."

"What'd you say?" Missy asked.

"I told them both that the way God teaches forgiveness is He gives us something to forgive."

"So how's that going?" Dora asked.

C3 answered before Christine or Sarah could. "A work in progress."

Sarah got up, went to the refrigerator, and returned with a beer. She took a juice box from the bag she'd brought along, stuck a straw through the hole in its top, and handed it to Livvie, who took it, sipped, then turned to Missy.

"Doddy hoot," she said, her expression intense.

"I know," Missy answered, compassion in her voice. "Daddy's hurt, but he's getting better."

"Bettaww," Livvie replied, after considering Missy's words.

Comfort ran out of the room. Freedom followed.

"I explained to C that life is too short to not speak to family. My mother and her sister, my Aunt Rona, stopped speaking for some reason nobody remembers, and died without ever speaking again."

"Maybe they were onto something," C3 commented.

Christine said to him, "You and I are alike in one way. We're the only ones in the family who believe in God. Isn't that right?"

C3 nodded, conceding the point. "I have to if I want to stay sober."

"So act like it. Charlie's desperate to see his granddaughter."

Charlie had returned with his glass of scotch. "I wouldn't say desperate."

"He can see Livvie, but my contact with him's going to be limited," C3 said.

"Hey, son. I'm right here."

"I know it, Pop. Can't miss you."

Sarah glared at C3. "He's your father!"

"I'm going to try to forget that," C3 said, looking away.

"How can you—you're just like him!"

Comfort trotted into the room, a pair of women's panties in his mouth. The dog sat in the middle of the circle of people and began licking the inside of the panties. Freedom tried to nose her way into the action, but Comfort angled his body, to force the much bigger dog away.

"Oh, my God," Missy said, mortified. She pulled the panties away, and hurried from the room, with Comfort on her heels.

Everyone laughed.

Epilogue

The following morning, Dora woke up to the sound of Missy speaking in low, concerned tones on her cell.

"I don't see any alternative, really, assuming he's going to live with you. Someone's got to keep an eye on him." Dora sat up and Missy, who was at the desk on the other side of the bedroom, gave her a faint smile.

"Okay," Missy said. "What time?" She listened. "Of course, I'll be there. Yes. See you then." She ended the call and looked at Dora, her expression stern and far away. "So my father's been going out at night and wandering around the neighborhood, picking things out of other people's garbage and bringing them home. Toaster ovens, kids' toys—all sorts of crap."

"Whoa," Dora said. "What are they going to do?"

"He's living with my sister and her husband. That was Bai, just now. She's freaking out."

Dora nodded slowly but said nothing. What was there to say?

"He's also taking stuff from our house and bringing it out to the street as garbage, and sometimes adding it to other people's garbage. He took my sister's guitar and her husband's iPhone." She looked at Dora, and when Dora didn't respond, she said, "They really need my help. They're having a get-together—they're calling it a party—in the back of the Beach City Diner this afternoon."

"Right. So you're going."

"Of course, I'm going."

"Well, I understand, but please understand how I feel about this stuff."

"You feel…"

"Left out. Kind of abandoned, seeing as how I have no one but you, and you have this family."

Missy took a breath and exhaled noisily. "So, you've said."

"What? You don't believe—"

"I'd like you to come."

"…me? Wait, what? You'd like me to come? To your family party? I won't be intruding?"

Missy shook her head. "You're never intruding. Yes, I want you to come."

"You're sure?"

• • •

Several hours later, Dora and Missy walked into the Beach City Diner and explained to the maître d' that they were attending the party in the back room. They wound their way between tables to the doorway that opened into the back room, which was used for private parties.

As the door opened, Dora was surprised to see balloons and streamers everywhere—on all of the walls and the ceiling. The tables all had beautiful floral centerpieces, which were also decorated with balloons and streamers, along with a photo in the center of each one.

The photo was of Dora and Missy—their private anniversary photo from the previous year.

The room was filled with seventy-five people—Missy's family and friends of the family. "Surprise!" everyone in the room yelled at once and instantly crowded around Dora and Missy.

Dora was stunned and bewildered. She had no idea what was happening, but Missy quickly remedied that by turning to her and saying, "Welcome to our family!" and kissing her hard, on the mouth.

• • •

They drove home happy and well-fed, though they had each perhaps eaten too much cake.

While they were driving, Dora's phone rang. A name appeared on the dashboard display and the two investigators looked at one another; Dora widened her eyes and nodded. Missy pressed a button on the display.

"Katie, hi!" Dora said.

"I won't keep you," Katie Drucker said. "I just wanted to let you know two things. First, thank you. Thank you so much! And second, you're paid in full."

"You're very welcome, Katie," Dora said.

"We're so happy we could help," Missy added. Katie ended the call.

As they entered their building's parking lot, Dora said, "I've got something to show you. Remember when I said I had my own idea for dealing with depression?"

Missy looked confused. "I do, but I thought you were talking about going to the gym and fighting—or maybe that wild fight you and Long got into at the P&W."

"Well, those fights helped, but no, I was talking about something else."

Dora pulled the rest of the way into the parking lot, got out of the car, and waited for Missy, who continued to look baffled.

Dora led her to the opposite side of the lot where, under a fire escape, against the side of the building, a brand-new Harley Davidson motorcycle gleamed in the sun. Dora stood next to it, grinning.

Missy stared at her. "This—is yours?"

Dora's grin widened. "Yup—and guess who's riding pillion. Do you know what pillion means?"

Missy looked at Dora with mock disdain. "I'm a fucking librarian. I know what pillion means. It's the passenger seat behind the driver."

Dora's mouth twisted in mock dismay. "My potty mouth is rubbing off on someone."

"So you expect me to ride with you on this thing?" Missy asked, her eyes wide and eyebrows raised.

"Yup," Dora said. "Off into the sunset."

THE END

Dear Reader: Thanks so much for reading A Divisive Storm.
I hope you will join my mailing list to learn more about my books at:
https://www.davidefeldman.com/books.shtml
If you enjoyed this book, I would be grateful if you would
post a review online.
See you again soon!
-DF

www.ingramcontent.com/pod-product-compliance
Lightning Source LLC
Chambersburg PA
CBHW061511120726
48001CB00004B/1290